The nightmare confusion was straining her yet untested inner strength. Hands rigid against her trim thighs, her mouth was open in a scream that melded into the racket like a piccolo entry. She saw Helena and stumbled to her through the debris. As Helena took her hands to try to calm her, there was a dramatic change.

All sound died away. The frenzied light storm ebbed to a white calm.

They had reached the still dead center, a time-less no-man's-land. . . .

MOON ODYSSEY
was originally published by Futura Publications Limited.

Books in the Space: 1999 Series

Breakaway
Moon Odyssey

Published by POCKET BOOKS

MOON
ODYSSEY

JOHN RANKINE

PUBLISHED BY POCKET BOOKS NEW YORK

MOON ODYSSEY

Futura Publications edition published 1975

POCKET BOOK edition published September, 1975

2nd printing.....................September, 1975

ᴌ

This POCKET BOOK edition includes every word contained in the original, higher-priced edition. It is printed from brand-new plates made from completely reset, clear, easy-to-read type. POCKET BOOK editions are published by POCKET BOOKS, a division of Simon & Schuster, Inc., 630 Fifth Avenue, New York, N.Y. 10020. Trademarks registered in the United States and other countries.

Standard Book Number: 671-80185-6.

MOON
ODYSSEY

CHAPTER ONE

Commander John Koenig stood looking out of the window of his executive suite and reckoned irritably that the fever which was affecting all personnel on Moonbase Alpha had finally gotten round to him. He could see into Main Mission and even without sound he could see every last one of the duty crew behaving like an expectant father in a vaudeville sketch. Anybody would think no woman had ever produced a child before and given the teeming millions on Earth planet it was plain ludicrous.

He saw his own face reflected on the glass and superimposed on the picture. Lines were deepening. Maybe he was just getting old and the recurring miracle of human birth no longer touched him? One thing was for sure, he was turning into a autocratic bastard. Any day now some hard pressed crewman would plant a pick in his skull. But he had to do it. He had to drive them. Keep a sense of purpose even if that purpose turned into a hatred of himself.

High forehead, square jaw, beak of a nose, black skull cap of hair, he should have been a hard case mate in the piping days of sail. The parallel ended there. At least on a windjammer the crew would know there was a landfall somewhere ahead. He was skipper of a rudderless hulk going nowhere at a mind-bending speed.

Red Alert klaxons sounded out through the complex

and reflection cut off. Suddenly, he was as anxious as the next man to see Cynthia Crawford's contribution to the life force. Koenig said, 'That's it,' and whipped out his commlock to open the hatch to Mission Control.

Paul Morrow, sitting at the conference table lifted his head out of his hands and was only a pace behind his chief as they entered the big control spread.

The atmosphere had changed to instant celebration. It was clear that everybody had felt involved. Paul Morrow, chief executive of Main Mission wore a grin that threatened to split his sandy head as he said, 'We made it!' Sandra Benes swinging elegant legs as she turned in her operation's chair said 'I like that! Whatever did you do to help?'

Koenig was tuning the main scanner and brought in the medicentre with Helena Russell looking wide-eyed and more pleased than she had done for months. Still in a theatre gown with the face mask dropped round her neck, she announced the first Moonbase national, 'It's a boy. Mother and baby doing just fine. Crawford Junior came in at four pounds three ounces. Fair hair, blue eyes—he's beautiful.'

Morrow said, 'There you are, a boy. I knew it. I knew it.' Koenig, warming to the holiday spirit that was clearly bursting out all over, looked ten years younger. But truth was truth, 'You had a bet with me it'd be a girl.'

'Never.'

In the medicentre itself Helena Russell had gone back to the bedside and was talking to her patient, 'You have a fine son, Cynthia. Sleep now. I'll let you see him later.'

'Thank you, Doctor.'

Cynthia Crawford was the only one not smiling. 'I only wish Jack had been alive to see him.'

8

'I know, I know. But life goes on. You've proved that for all of us. Get some sleep. That's an order.'

Helena turned to her team. Bob Mathias was at the monitors and Paula carefully settled the new boy in his incubator, 'Ready Bob?'

Mathias flipped switches and watched the screens put up a diagnostic check-out. He said 'No complications.'

'Well done both of you. But I think he should be under constant watch. You two take a spell. I'll do first stint.'

Paula was off like a lissom rocket, but Mathias held back. She said again 'Go on Bob. I'm not really tired. Anyway I don't want to leave. This is a medical first.'

She drew up a chair and looked at the baby, chin on hand, wide spaced eyes dreamy. It was a good thing to have done. The best. Skill used to create rather than mend the pieces. Behind her, the wave patterns on the scopes began to increase. Far away, outside the confines of the quiet room and not yet picked up by receptors in Mission Control a distant green speck was pulsing to the same tempo.

Helena crossed to Cynthia Crawford, picked her wrist from the coverlet and did a check with her time disk. Old fashioned medicine, but it was very satisfying. She was still following that line in her head, when the monitors whipped over the threshold of attention with a succession of urgent blips.

She looked first at the incubator and the whole sand castle of euphoria crumbled around her. Hand to her mouth, suddenly sick with shock she could only back away until she felt the cold wall of the bulkhead against her shoulders. Only Cynthia Crawford's urgent repeated screams broke the numb circle of horror and drove her forward to pull a screen round the transparent bubble. But the image was etched forever in her mind.

The body in the incubator had gone into explosive growth. The face and body were pressed grotesquely against the glass. It was no longer a tiny helpless baby. It was a boy, a five-year-old at the least.

John Koenig reckoned bitterly that they should have known better than to expect anything good to come their way. He was more sorry for Helena than for anybody. She had been so proud of her skill and so deeply happy. She deserved better. In the medicentre Nurse Paula was fussing round the boy who seemed docile, almost serene who looked steadily at him as he put an arm on Helena's shoulders, and he asked quietly, 'Is there any explanation, anything at all that occurs to you?'

Helena Russell shook her head miserably, 'How can there be? In normal terms he's physically about five years old. And it happened in a matter of seconds. Cell growth accelerated beyond belief.'

'But how? What are the cells composed of? He's taken no food. How can he grow without protein? Without vitamins?'

'Not only that. There's motor control. Even a simple thing like sitting erect is the result of a learning process. Co-ordination comes by experience. How can he have had that experience? How can he be as normal as he appears? There can be no rational explanation.'

'Irrational, then?'

'John, don't rush me. I'm just trying to come to terms with something outside our terms of reference.'

Koenig tried a personal approach, crossed to the cot that Paula had set up and tried to make his voice sound natural. 'Hello, young fella.' He reached out and touched the child's hand, remembering that physical contact spoke clearer than words. It produced a quick smile and he found himself smiling back. Maybe after the initial teething troubles, if that was the right phrase, the kid would be okay? He gave the hand another pat to signal that only friendship was intended and then rejoined Helena looking thoughtful.

'Helena it's impossible.'

'We knew there might be problems but . . .' she trailed off, unable to find words for the trick fate had played them.

'Jack Crawford's death made it seem like a good idea.'

'It *was* good. It was *right*. But now it's all come out wrong. I'll do every test I know, but I can't say what to expect, what to look for.'

Koenig cut in, 'Jack Crawford, the father. You never went along with the theory that he died of cell mutation.'

'I don't *know* why he died. At times we have to accept the unknown. But I can positively say it was *not* cell mutation.'

'All the same I'll take another look at the Nuclear Generating Plant.'

'I'll work on those tests.'

At the plant, technician Joan Conway, a neat, supple figure in a rust brown inner suit was immediately suspicious—

'But Jack Crawford died seven months ago, Commander. What is it? Is there something wrong with our baby?'

'I'm afraid there is. And I'm trying to find out what caused it. Jack Crawford spent most of his working life in here.'

'But they pulled this place apart when he died. There was no radiation leakage.' Kohl rimmed eyes opened wide, 'Is it mutation?'

'Of a kind.'

Any reply was lost in a buzz from the communications post and Helena's face appeared on the scanner.

'John?'

'Here.'

'Tests show he's normal. A normal five-year-old child.'

Simultaneously screened in Main Mission it caused a shocked silence. Carter the chief pilot expressed a general feeling when he said bitterly, 'Maybe we had no right to expect anything else.'

Sandra Benes said, 'You mean we can never expect to have normal children?'

'This crazy kind of life we lead. No-one really knows how it's affecting us physically—or in the long term.'

Paul Morrow could see morale taking a plunge. He said, 'Come on. Life here's not that abnormal. We eat, drink, sleep, breathe air of a kind. Maybe it's some specific cause in this case.'

Carter said, 'Like Crawford's death?'

At the computer spread, Kano called over, 'They're asking for data on the Nuclear Generating Plant. Looks like the Commander's re-opening the enquiry.'

Carter gave it a cynical twist, 'Like the command manual says—always do something. I guess he has to go through the motions.'

In the medical unit Helena Russell was unconsciously following the same precept. When Koenig appeared through the hatch, she had the prodigy in a diagnostic chair and was busy peeling off the sensors which had been planted on his limbs and temples.

Mathias looked worried and was checking his note pad. 'Brain activity is no more and certainly no less than you'd expect in a five-year-old human male.'

'That means he's thinking.'

'But not communicating.'

'How could he be? He's had no chance to learn to speak. Yet he seems so alert—so responsive.'

Talking it out triggered a recall of a simple test she had seen in medical school. She picked up a flask and attracted the child's attention. As she moved it his eyes followed it, trying to guess what she was at. Mathias picked up the cue and moved quietly behind the chair picking up a couple of kidney bowls on the way. Helena gave a nod and he threw them to the floor with a clang that made Paula skip like a Spring lamb. But the child was watching Helena's flask and neither blinked nor turned away.

Koenig said, 'Deaf mute?'

Helena was firm, 'But he's *here*. He exists. He's *our* responsibility. Our first concern is how we aim to handle him.'

'You'd be happy doing that?'

'Surely. I'll give Cynthia all the help she needs. We have to do the best we can for him. Later, we may or may not find out why it happened this way.'

'So, as of now, we try to give him as normal a life as possible.'

'However it happened, it happened. We're left with an apparently normal child. A lovely child. You can see he's going to be the spitting image of Jack. That should be a great thing for Cynthia, when she comes to accept it.'

'If she comes to accept it.'

'Why do you say that?'

Koenig looked apologetic, 'Sorry. I just don't know. I have a curious feeling about him that I can't put a finger on.'

'Well, it's time he was introduced to company. The sooner everybody realises we haven't produced a monster the better. Ignorance is fear.'

'After all it's his birthday.'

It earned him a burning look and he followed her

through into Main Misson as she walked the child by the hand.

She was right on one count. The atmosphere was already tense. Every eye tracked them into a stunned silence. Only the ongoing electronic mush from the computer spread filled the background.

Carter broke it, working hard to be genial. The child pushed hard against Helena's smooth thigh as the pilot came near and stared hard with simple fear as Carter gave him a friendly poke and asked, 'What's your name, youngster?'

There was no reply. Helena said, 'We've called him Jackie.'

'Hi then, Jackie. How'd you like to go for a flight? We'll take an Eagle and soar around.'

He was doing his best, making flying mimes with both hands. Helena said quietly, 'He can't hear you, Alan.'

Alan Carter stopped dead. Then compassion took over, 'No? The poor little devil. Then I'll just have to show him. Come on Jackie. Away we go.'

Holding the boy over his head Carter did a circuit of Mission Control. Simple stuff and harking back in memory to many an apartment on Earth planet. Whether Jackie understood it or not, he was reassured by the warm physical contact. He was smiling and the likeness to Jack Crawford was obvious. It was infectious. Reservations melted. When Carter took him back to Helena there was a new feeling in the group.

Koenig had gone through into his office and was watching the dumb show and saw that it would turn out well. They were good people. They would do what they could for the boy. He saw Helena take Jackie over to Paul Morrow and the Main Mission Controller gave the boy his commlock and showed him the operating button. Between them they directed the beam to his own door and he went along with the game meeting them on the steps as Morrow said, 'Commander. We have a visitor.'

Koenig and Helena led him between them and sat him in the command chair and Koenig called to Kano. 'David. Give us something colourful to look at.'

Geometric patterns in blue and green and gold came up on the main scanner. Koenig altered it, using the controls on his own desk and Jackie watched intently, pressing another himself for a second change.

Helena said, 'You see. There's no doubt about his intelligence.'

Jackie was absorbed and his face was serious with concentration as he checked over every control on the panel.

The doubt he could not quite suppress, rose again in Koenig's head. His own face set in a stern mask and the child sensed it as disapproval. He stopped his play and tears welled in his eyes and he turned away to hide his face on Helena's chest.

There was no doubt it made a difference having a youngster in the complex. All hands took a delight in showing him how things worked. Professor Bergman took time off from a piece of research he had lined up and tried speech training. With a large coloured spread of a buttercup from a natural history book in front of them, he touched Jackie's face to draw attention from the page and then touched the boy's lips and his own to make a visual bond. With elaborate lips movements he said, 'Fl-ow-er. Fl-ow-er.'

He got some response. Jackie watched it through and smiled, but something had caught his eye. As Bergman searched for another easy picture, he was looking over his shoulder at the maze of scientific equipment and his eyes, if Bergman could have seen them, were anything but childlike. Even at the distance, he was working it out. He *knew* what was being done.

Helena took him about, letting him see every department of his new home. In the Nuclear Generating Plant, Joan Conway made him welcome, picking him up and sitting him on her shoulders for a tour of inspection. 'Who's his father's son, then? My you're doing fine, finding out all about your uncles and aunts. He's a good solid weight.'

'Thirty eight pounds. Absolutely normal.'

The eyes over their heads were ranging round the site with a look of uncanny interest and understanding.

Carter made him a model mock up of an Eagle and the boy took it all in with concentration and seriousness that was lost on the pilot as he got absorbed in his own game.

The only one who would have nothing at all to do with him was Cynthia Crawford. She had relapsed into a coma-like state, but any attempt to bring Jackie close to her produced a frenzy and agitation that could not be pacified until he was taken out.

Helena took Koenig along to see her.

'She's completely rejected the child.'

'I suppose that's an understandable reaction.'

'Everybody else on Alpha's taken to him. But she's refusing to come out of this state of shock. She won't let him come near. I get the feeling that if only I could show her how he's leading a comparatively normal life. . . .'

'It's *how* he reached that stage that's disturbing. I have to say I still can't accept that either.'

'Where is he now?'

'I saw him with Bergman as I came through.'

'That's all right. Victor's good with him. I believe if anybody can get him to talk it will be Victor. He has marvellous sympathy and patience.'

'I like to watch him at it. I'll join them. You take a break. You give all your time to him.'

Bergman had Jackie Crawford beside him at his desk and they were still flogging at the buttercup. Jackie was making a bad copy, but Bergman never stopped giving praise.

'That's good Jackie. Very good. Would you like to do another?'

He set up a fresh sheet of paper as his commlock buzzed from the desk. Quick as a flash Jackie reached over and pressed the right button. Koenig's face glowed on the miniature screen.

Following the correct sequence Jackie picked another stud and the doors opened to admit Koenig himself.

'He's making progress, Victor.'

'John, there's not a doubt about it. He's bright. Very bright.'

Koenig leaned over the table and spoke quietly close to Bergman's head. 'You're sure?'

'As I read him, he's perfectly normal.'

'Is he Victor? Is he? We want to believe it. I think our critical faculties might have been put to sleep by young Jackie's charm.'

He would have been more sure of that if he had seen the boy's eyes. He would have known for a start that the conversation was being heard and understood.

Bergman said, 'So he's still under observation?'

'He has to be Victor.'

Both looked at the boy who was now only looking at his drawing. Trying hard to be friendly, Koenig said, 'Let me look. What have you been drawing?'

As he stretched out a hand for the paper, Jackie quickly crumpled it in a tight ball.

Bergman laughed, 'Young children are like young animals John. They have an extra keen sense about

17

people. He knows you're not as willing to take him at face value as the rest of us.'

Koenig's commlock buzzed urgently and he missed the look that Jackie Crawford was giving it. There was expectation there as though he knew the message before Paul Morrow's concerned face on the miniature screen could deliver it.

'Commander. Will you come into Main Mission at once please?'

'Right away.'

There was activity all around. The full staff were on the floor. Morrow said, 'Sandra. Give me a reading.'

'Velocity two seven five and closing.'

Koenig was behind his chair watching the console.

'Scanner's on to something, Commander. Heading right for us.'

Alan Carter whistled, 'Only look at that! By god it's moving fast!'

Koenig called, 'Kano?'

'Nothing yet from the computer, Commander.'

'Let's have it on the main scanner.'

Paul Morrow threw switches. There was the familiar star map and the infinite corridors of space-time; random alleys for their Moon ball to rattle in. But something new, a feature with a harmonic of menace, even before it crystalised out into a recognisable artifact. There was a throbbing pulse of viridian light coming in on a collision course and moving with unbelievable speed.

Morrow asked, 'Red Alert?'

'Red Alert.'

Klaxons sounded out and red tell tales winked in every corner of the complex. The green light was shaking out into definition. It was a spacer of unfamiliar pattern, though they could have had a preview of it if anybody had uncurled the tight ball of paper

18

in Bergman's waste bin. Jackie Crawford had already drawn it out to the last fluted dome.

Paul Morrow had a directional fix. 'It's headed for the North quadrant, Commander.'

Koenig left the group to see it live from the external vision ports. Alan Carter joined him. There was the spread of the complex as clear as day under the floods and the huge bulk of the spacer hovering over the perimeter markers of the North Quadrant. Morrow left the scanner, then Kano. They all lined up at the direct vision ports as if to convince themselves that it was true and not something cooked up by micro gremlins in the hardware.

For the first time since his birth, Jackie Crawford was not the centre of attention. He walked in from Koenig's office and stood at the back of the line. Then he looked round Main Mission with adult, intelligent eyes like a new manager taking a sneak preview of the general office while the staff was out on a coffee break.

There was no doubt about the air of menace, but there was no communication. Koenig came to a decision and pulled Carter out of the ruck. Jackie Crawford followed them through into the command office and sat silent looking from one face to the other as Koenig briefed his chief pilot for a reconnaissance mission.

When it was done, Koenig stood up. He knew what he was asking and he didn't like any part of it. 'All right, Alan. You know what to do.'

'And if I'm attacked?'

'Don't wait for me to give the order.'

Koenig was not the only one who disliked sending Carter out. As the pilot turned to go, the boy ran to his side and took his arm as though to hold him back. Koenig said, 'Good luck, Alan,' but Carter was side-tracked by Jackie's obvious worry. He ruffled

19

the boy's hair, leaned down and said clearly, 'I'll be back.'

There was no change. The boy either did not understand or did not believe it. Carter went down to a full knee bend that brought their heads on a level and really worked at it, 'It's—all—right, I'll—be—back.'

There was still no joy. Koenig said, 'Here Jackie,' and made a beckoning mime that was impossible to miss. 'Here. We'll watch from my desk.'

It earned him a curious look which was only partly agreement. There was an element in it which said, 'All right then, Commander. Just for now I'll do what you want. But not for long. Not for very long. Soon, I shall be telling you.'

They saw Carter gun his motor and lift his Eagle in a surge of power off the pad. Then he was doing a discreet circuit of the spacer. Koenig had all personnel back at stations and had forgotten Jackie Crawford still sitting quietly at his desk.

He called through to Kano, 'What's holding you? I want computer analysis of that spacer.'

'Coming through now, Commander.'

Koenig looked at the blow up on the main scanner, 'It's in advance of anything we have, but it looks as though the evolution of design has gone along a path we know. That points to an intelligence we would recognise.' Paul Morrow said, 'I agree, Commander. But why don't they communicate?'

'Keep trying on all channels. Monitor all frequencies for any kind of response. Anything.'

He switched to the roving Eagle and Carter's command module came up on his screen with Carter and his co-pilot staring fixedly ahead. 'Any sign of action, Alan?'

'Not a thing, Commander. Except the flicker on this green light. Comes from the dome, right on top.

There's no movement. They're just hanging there like a putrified marrow.'

'You hang right in there with them. Report any sign of life.'

'Check. I'm going in closer. We'll let you know if they fire. Three knocks on the table.'

A blip from Kano's desk had Koenig reluctantly switching channels.

Kano swivelled in his seat with a print-out in his hand and said, 'It's made of an alloy, but we don't have any matching symbols for the composition. It's one hundred metres in diameter, forty metres high, but it has this fantastically low density.'

'You're telling me there's room for a battalion in there.'

'Computer finds some life form indicated, but not human. Computer is insufficiently programmed to identify it.'

Paul Morrow cut in, 'They could blast us at any second if it suited their book. Why should they give any warning?'

'Maybe they've done the same kind of breakdown and like us they're waiting for the other side to make the first move.'

'Either way, their behaviour is suspicious.'

Sandra Benes supported her chief, 'If they're friendly, they only have to say so.'

Morrow checked on the Eagle. 'Alan's real close, Commander. I think we should make the first move.'

Information was crowding Koenig's network. Carter himself came through, 'I have it lined up, Commander. Lasers set for maximum strike. I can't miss. Carve up that green dome for a sure thing.'

Morrow said, 'Better safe than sorry. I think we should do just that, Commander.'

Koenig looked from screen to screen. Carter and Morrow. The axeman and the advisor. But the final say had to be his. It was the ultimate loneliness of command to have the life or death decision.

Jackie Crawford had moved round the desk and his eyes were fixed on Koenig's face in a steady penetrating stare as though he knew precisely what was going on in the Commander's head and had a personal stake in it.

Koenig was suddenly sidetracked. Beyond the child's face he could see Helena Russell and the care she had taken to preserve life. Intelligent life was rare enough in the wastes of space to have its right to survive. Who was he to pull the plug and wipe it out?

Somewhere in the subconscious where every man is a stranger to his own motivation, relays clicked and the decision was made. He spoke to Carter. 'Alan. Return to base.'

Shocked into protest, Carter's single word came back, 'Why?'

'They could have blasted you out of the sky. They didn't. They had every right to believe *you* were the aggressor.'

Paul Morrow intervened, voicing the doubt showing on every face in Main Mission. 'Commander. We're wide open. Maybe they're getting just everything they want by keeping quiet.'

Koenig ignored him, staying with Carter, trying to force conviction. 'See it their way, Alan. When we do a reconnaissance on an alien planet we try to communicate all we can. It's not out intention to attack. Maybe that ship holds peaceful people trying to make contact and we're just not hearing or understanding yet.'

'That's not my reading, Commander.'

'Ignorance is no reason to start shooting. We're all afraid of the unknown. As a matter of plain fact I'm scared of Jackie Crawford here.'

It was a sudden change of tack and he saw surprise and disbelief on every face as he went on, 'I know you've all come to accept him. But you've put aside the fact that we don't know why he's like he is. We can't explain it or understand it. For me that's still difficult to take. But I don't shoot him.'

'I follow that Commander. But I still think you have it wrong. Pulling out. Returning to base.'

Koenig passed a hand wearily over his forehead. He was suddenly very tired. He looked for Jackie Crawford to reassure him if the boy had picked up any overtones in the exchange and was feeling threatened; but he had wandered off.

He had gone where he was sure of a welcome and was in the medicentre sidling up to Helena Russell and taking her hand. She had been attending to Cynthia Crawford and they were not two metres from the bed when Cynthia opened her eyes.

Before Helena could speak, her face distorted with fear and her body arched violently from the bed. Mouth wide, she began to scream. 'No. Don't let him. Take him away. He's killing me.' She fell back racked by hysterical sobbing.

Mathias and Paula were quickly at her side, beating Helena to it. She said, 'Paula. I'll attend to her. Take Jackie out.'

As she handed him over, she stooped down to reassure him and was suddenly appalled. He was smiling. He knew what was happening to Cynthia: but it made no difference. He wanted it. For some reason he wanted it that way.

Cynthia's cries were more urgent. Helena joined Mathias. As they calmed her, Jackie Crawford waited for Paula to use her commlock on the medicentre hatch and then walked quickly out with a purposeful step which was all at odds with his child's shape.

Helena Russell felt she owed Koenig an apology.

She had been critical of his attitude; but now her eyes were open. As soon as Cynthia was quiet again she went to find him.

'John. It was horrible. There was something about the way he smiled. It sent a chill right through me. He *knew*. It was as though he were enjoying his mother's agony.'

'Where is he now?'

'I don't know. With Paula somewhere.'

Koenig called Morrow, 'Paul. Find Jackie Crawford and don't let him out of your sight.'

Helena looked defeated and he went round his desk and took her hands. 'Don't blame yourself. Everybody felt the same way about him. We all bent backwards to look for the good things, to accept him as normal. But now we know he's not. He's *too* bright. Too much charm. Like with a precocious child, he makes you feel uneasy. As though you were being judged.'

'He knew you had reservations.'

'Helena, he's fooled us all.'

Paul Morrow called urgently, 'Commander. Three more spacers running in to Alpha.'

Koenig was on the way as the Red Alert klaxons sounded out and he was saying to himself as much as to her, 'Maybe there's a connection?'

Sandra Benes looked white, 'Confirmed, Commander. Three more. Identical with the first.'

The main scanner had the picture. They were in echelon, closing fast with green lights in a pulsing triangle.

Koenig snapped out, 'Carter. Take three flights of Eagles and intercept.'

'Preventive mission?'

'No. Let them see we're ready for them. Where's Jackie?'

Helena saw him. He was on the balcony above

the operations floor. Koenig followed her eyes and saw the boy's fixed smile.

'Get to him Helena.'

At the same time, long streamers of green light seared out from the racing craft and the main scanner blanked out.

Morrow said, 'They've knocked out all cameras, Commander.'

Carter turned from the hatch and said definitively, 'It's an attack.'

Koenig saw Helena reach the boy and he saw the smile hardening into something like triumph. He said, 'Stop them, Alan.'

'Yes, sir.'

Carter too was looking at the boy and seemed to be suddenly beset by indecision. Koenig's shout, 'Move man! Get on with it,' tipped the scale and got him in motion again.

Koenig himself raced for the balcony and Jackie Crawford shook himself free of Helena's hand and stumbled backwards until he was brought up by the curved bulkhead at his back. Suddenly the smile faded. He looked like a trapped animal. Hands covering his face, he began to shake as though with pain. Slowly he dropped to his knees and then pitched forward face down.

Koenig said, 'All right, Helena. Get him into the medicentre. Keep him under watch.'

Through the direct vision ports on the balcony he saw Carter's squadron lifting off. One after another, six Eagles blasted from the strip and Carter took them in a tight formation into the path of the oncoming spacers.

Carter's voice came up on the commlock, 'Eagle leader to Alpha. Do you read me?'

Koenig said, 'Commander Alpha. I read you.'

'Alien space ships dead ahead.'

'Fire as you bear.'

There was no mistaking the relief in Alan Carter's voice.

'Now you're talking. Eagle leader to Eagle squadron. Select on-board ranging. Manual override. Fire as you bear.'

Through the direct vision port Koenig saw the thin beams flare out from the hurrying Eagles. Against all logic, there was not a hit. He said urgently, 'Switch to main computer. Check and fire.'

Carter's repetition was instant but carried a charge that sent a quick frown over Koenig's face. Carter said again, 'Manual override. Check and fire,' and a second pattern blossomed out with the lines bending away without penetration. Carter said angrily, 'It's no good. We can't get a hit.'

'Come in from behind. Maybe they have a blind quarter.'

The Eagles were turning, coming round to a new vector. Suddenly a volley of green rays streamed out from the spacers which had positioned themselves round the quadrants of the Alpha base. Each Eagle was bathed in a green glow. Koenig saw them check in flight and begin to float down to the moon's surface.

Main Mission had gone quiet. Everybody sat still, one question on every face. Outside, the four spacers hovered on station, their green domes pulsing with light. There was a feeling of impotence, a sense of waiting for something terrible to happen.

CHAPTER TWO

John Koenig stood at his command desk trying to
think it through. Being a hard critic of himself, he
was trying to pinpoint the place in time when the
situation had escalated out of control and when something he had done or not done had put the base under
this threat. Every time he came back to Jackie Crawford. In some way the key had to be there.

Maybe there was still something to be done? He
used his commlock to open his door and strode out
into Main Mission. All staff were still at action stations and he felt the weight of unspoken questions as
he went through without a word.

In the medicentre, Helena Russell was standing
in front of a monitoring console dividing her attention
between the scopes and a bank of flickering equipment
beyond a glass screen. Behind the screen in a cubicle
bathed in blue light, Jackie Crawford was lying under
a clutter of sophisticated support gear.

Noise from the monitors was building and Koenig
was behind her before she heard his step. As though
to stop something she could not bear to hear, she
flipped switches in a row to turn off audio repeaters
and there was instant silence.

She spoke to his reflection in the polished panelling,
'Cell growth has accelerated beyond the capacity of
our instruments to measure.'

'But still increasing?'

27

She nodded miserably, fair hair waving and Koenig was sidetracked by the perfect proportions of her face, its high cheekbones, the long smooth curve to the jaw, the line of the eyebrows. She was the best reason there was for finding a way out for them all. With an effort, he forced his mind to the problem. 'What do we expect this time? It's too much of a coincidence. The spacers home in, now this.'

'You think they had something to do with Jackie from the beginning?'

'I don't think it's going to help any of us to go on thinking of this,' he nodded to the figure behind the screen, 'as Jackie Crawford. There is some kind of alien presence amongst us and sooner or later we may have to destroy it.'

Helena Russell twisted round to take a square look at the owner of the reflection, not sure that she was reading facial clues aright. 'But John. What are you saying? It's a human being!'

'Is it?' Koenig's hands cupped her head as he said slowly, 'It has a *human* form. That's all we know. We're wide open. Time's run out for waiting to see what happens.'

'You remember the reasons for your first decision about Jackie? They still hold. We still don't know any more—good or bad. We're just more afraid, more desperate. It's a *subjective* judgement.'

Koenig's fingers felt the smooth pad of silky hair and he bent his arms to pull her towards him. For him it was crystal clear. He said, 'At this moment, Jackie Crawford or whatever he has become is a threat to our existence.'

Over his shoulder, Helena had a long view out through a direct vision port. One of the spacers was menacingly close. Gently but firmly she disengaged his hands and crossed to the window to make her point. 'Then the reasons for *not* destroying him are

28

even stronger. As you say, we're wide open. If he's *their* instrument how do you think they'll react if we kill him?'

Koenig's answer was oblique, but she knew he had seen the force of her argument. He spoke harshly into his commlock. 'Paul. Command Conference. Now.'

She watched his erect figure out through the hatch and hated herself for adding to his problems. When the door closed she joined Mathias and they both watched the monitor's insane chattering.

Koenig looked round the table at Kano, Paul Morrow and Carter and concluded his situation report. 'So, reluctantly, I have to agree with Dr Russell. At this moment in time, as far as Jackie Crawford is concerned, our hands are tied.'

Alan Carter said, 'That leaves the spacers themselves. As they're placed we wouldn't even get an Eagle up on the pad.'

'We couldn't be sure of an effective strike if we did.'

The pilot shifted uneasily in his chair. He knew what Koenig was getting at. Koenig left him in no doubt, 'I'm not sure you could handle it, Alan. You loused up that attack. But I don't happen to believe you'd make that kind of error in your right mind.'

'It was the computer.'

'Was it?'

'What are you saying, Commander?'

'Believe me, I'm not fixing the blame. I think you were got at by Jackie.'

Carter was bitter, 'Yeah, well. We're all awake to him now Commander.'

'Like I said, I'm not blaming you. As I see it we can only hope that they'll hold on fast on their green ray transmissions. If and when that happens we can go to work.'

'Doing what?'

'This may be primitive and we'll need darkness. But I suggest a small party on foot. Four men. Each equipped with hand held armour piercing lasers. They move into position, one below each ship. Time it to a second and fire simultaneously.'

Kano whistled, 'You said it was primitive!'

Morrow put it in perspective, 'What else can we do?'

Koenig made the decision, 'Right. All that remains is to set it up. There are four of us here.'

As if on cue, Sandra Benes buzzed on the communications post and spoke quietly. 'Commander the green lights have stopped.'

It was true. Checking from the vision ports, Koenig could see the huge spacers hovering North, West, South and East like containing cliffs. Their domes were still flushed with a weird green glow but the pulsations had stopped.

Koenig said, 'This is it. There may be no other chance. We go now. Alan, West. Kano, South. Paul, East. I'll take North. Count down from my commlock. Good luck.'

Action cleared his head. As he stepped out of the North lock, a bulky anonymous figure in full space gear, carrying a heavy manual laser, he felt that at last the initiative had shifted to the Alpha party. Using his commlock, he watched the others make their exits and moved off to position himself under the huge belly of the spacer hovering a hundred metres over the North quadrant.

In the Intensive Care Unit, Helena Russell and Bob Mathias rounded the screen to take a closer look at the body in the life support tent. Helena wheeled back the covers, forcing herself to treat the problem in medical terms and stopped, hands falling to her sides, eyes suddenly enormous. Instead of Jackie Crawford, they had gotten a grown man, aged, if that had any meaning, about the middle forties, fair-haired and opening piercingly intelligent eyes as she and Mathias backed off in shock.

He sat up, cleared away the rest of the gear and stood up, using the sheet as a robe. Before they could reach the door, he spoke in a firm authoritative voice, 'My name is Jarak. For as long as you shall know me I shall retain this form. I require to know what has been happening during my period of growth.'

Helena found her voice, 'There are many things we'd like to know also.'

Jarak walked towards her, 'Has any action been taken against my space ships?'

Too quickly Helena said, 'None.'

'I know the truth when I hear it.'

'There's nothing we can do.'

Jarak reached her. Watching his eyes Helena felt resolution draining out of her. He took her wrists and his eyes seemed to be filling her mind. His voice seemed to be speaking from inside her head. 'Dr Russell, you *will* tell me.'

Mathias had come to her side and Jarak dropped her wrists, looking grim faced from one to the other. Slowly her hands lifted, crawled to the collar of Mathias's tunic, clamped definitively round his throat. Her face white with a struggle she could not resolve, she began to strangle him, with Mathias unable to move to help himself. Locked in horror she could only jerk out, 'Stop. I will tell you.' But the grip was tightening. Mathias was falling. Jarak said, 'Quickly or he dies.'

Helena was shouting in despair. 'Four men. Outside now. Stop.'

Her hands fell away and she looked at them in disbelief, hair hanging over her face.

Outside, Koenig was set and had his commlock on the count. Kano, Morrow and Carter had the repeat.

31

Each looked up to the lowering underbelly of a spacer. Digits whipped through the panels 32. 31. 30.

Jarak shrugged into an Alpha medicentre jacket and said coldly, 'And now *you* will stop them.'

'One life against three hundred, that's no deal.'

But her body had already sold the pass. Her hands had the commlock from her belt.

Mathias tried. Forcing himself to move her he reached out to grab it from her, but Jarak was between them taking his wrists and forcing him to meet his eyes. As Mathias fell, Helena was raising her commlock to speak.

Koenig saw digits flip down from 6 to 5. He put his commlock between his feet, raised his laser and had first pressure on the stud when an urgent blip had him lowering the aim and scooping up the communicator. Helena's frantic face on the miniature screen said, 'Stop, John, or Alpha will be destroyed.'

'Helena? Helena?'

But the screen had blanked. Moving fast, he sent out a general call. 'Hold it. Hold your fire.'

It was the bitterest moment he had ever had. He could imagine Carter's reaction, saw them in his mind's eye turning away from a sitting target. Paul Morrow called in 'What's the problem, Commander?'

Koenig was already moving, 'Return to base.'

Alan Carter said, 'Come all over peaceful again have they, Commander?'

He could not see Jarak's humourless smile or he would have had his answer.

But Jarak was at least using a polite form of words. He said to Helena, 'You have my thanks. Now I require to see Cynthia Crawford.'

Medical concern steadied her, 'She's not well enough to receive visitors.'

Jarak said patiently, 'Doctor, as a child you cared for me, even gave me human love. Believe me, I do not like to have to treat Alphans this way.' Helena still hesitated and his tone hardened, 'Now take me to her.'

Life support monitors showed that Moonbase Alpha's first mother was losing her lonely battle to stay alive. Against all expectation her eyes opened wide as they approached the bed and fixed fearfully on Jarak's face.

Mathias jerked out, 'Doctor, she's dying.' As they watched, the scopes faltered and the lines flattened. Helena Russell said, 'You've killed her.'

But Jarak was still staring into the blank open eyes. Without breaking the bond he said, 'Does computer confirm the death of Cynthia Crawford?'

There was a two second pause before the computer answered for itself, 'Cynthia Crawford, Deceased.'

Helena leaned over automatically and closed Cynthia's eyes. Then she went on blindly to a vision port and looked out. Eyes filled with tears she could see a green light pulsing from the nearest spacer. It was the end of their high hopes. Jarak was a monster. She turned to face him, ready to accuse him and was sidetracked by Cynthia herself.

Cynthia Crawford was revitalised. Hair piled regally on top of her head, face made up like an exquisitely beautiful doll, she was stirring, sitting up, holding out her hands, saying 'Jarak!'

'Rena!'—he pulled her to her feet and held her close kissing her throat, her eyes and finally her pouting mouth.

Laser ready, John Koenig moved cautiously into the corridor leading to Alpha's medicentre and checked that Morrow and his party were ready at the other intersection. He signalled to the two security details at his back and moved forward. The door of the medicentre sliced open and Helena Russell herself walked straight out.

Koenig ran forward. She turned like a zombie raising her right arm and he stopped. Her laser was aimed steadily at his head.

Morrow and his section were coming along like a train and she had to shout, 'Stop, Paul or I shoot.'

Koenig held out his hand and moved slowly. 'Helena, give me that.'

For a second, he thought she would respond then the laser shifted briefly off target and fired a single burst into a ceiling light over his head. There was a percussive crack and Koenig stopped motionless as the barrel came back to aim.

Helena said, 'Put down your weapons. There, by the door.'

When it was done the door slid open. Jarak and Rena stepped out side by side. Helena's action was understandable, but not their transformation. Koenig was still staring in disbelief at Rena as Jarak walked up to him and took his commlock, then stooped and helped himself to a laser. 'In Alpha we must do as the Alphans do.'

Rena walked in front of Helena, took the laser from her hand and stared into her eyes, 'Thank you, Doctor Russell. You are released.'

Helena passed her hands over her face and was swaying on her feet. Koenig went forward, put his arm round her shoulders. Trying to get it right he said to Rena, 'You're not Cynthia Crawford?'

Jarak said, 'No more than I am Jackie Crawford and no more than you are any longer Commander of Moonbase Alpha. We will all go along to the command office. Now, if you please.'

It was not until he was sitting at the command desk with Rena beside him and the staff of Main Mission disarmed and ready to listen that he was ready to speak again. John Koenig and Helena were at the foot of the steps, symbolically demoted. On the top step a pile of weapons sat under Jarak's penetrating eyes.

He said, 'Like you we are involuntary travellers through space. But unlike you we are looking not only for a place to live but also for a physical form to conceal our identity.'

Koenig said, 'Why? Are you trying to escape from something?'

'I appreciate the intuitive quality of your human mind, Commander. I also like your unpredictable human emotions. I like the differences that exist between you. On our planet, we faced extinction, because we were different. We are escaping from genetic conformity, ruthlessly imposed. We are happy to have found Alpha.'

He smiled, looking as though he expected everybody would be equally pleased but Koenig put him right, 'But you can't stay here. We cannot support your people. Our resources are precariously balanced. We can scarcely sustain ourselves.'

'Be sure I appreciate the problem. The population of Alpha will not increase. We shall simply take over your bodies and make them our own. The moments of birth and death are ideally suited to this purpose. It was the birth of Jackie Crawford that gave me my chance.'

There was more to it than that and Helena Russell blurted it out.

'But *you* killed Cynthia.'

Rena as the beneficiary answered that, 'Doctor Russell. There will be no more births on Alpha. But sadly there will be many more deaths.'

It caused a stir in the audience but Jarak went on impassively, 'I was happy with my birth. I was restricted in an incubator, but as a five year old you gave me free run of the base. You showed me all

I needed to know. I am truly sorry to bite the hands that fed me.'

John Koenig had heard enough. Deliberately he set himself to walk forward and went on although both Jarak and Rena raised lasers in warning. At point blank range, he stopped, 'You need us Jarak. I don't know what your people look like but I know they need us alive. You dare not kill us until you are ready.'

Jarak's smile had set coldly, 'We are ready.'

'But how much use will I be with a laser burn through my heart?' Koenig held out his hand, staring across the table into Jarak's eyes.

Slowly Jarak transferred the laser to his free hand and offered it across the desk butt first, saying at the same time, 'We are fighting to preserve our individuality, Commander. But no individual is more valuable than the community.'

It was a double edged comment and Helena realised what he intended as Koenig's hand turned the laser against himself. She started forward in fear, 'No, Jarak. Don't make him do it.'

Rena met her, jamming her own laser into her chest, saying icily, 'We will kill you all if we must.'

Koenig's forefinger was on the stud, he could only wait like any spectator for the killing shot. An unarmed security man, forgotten by Jarak dived desperately to shove the barrel aside and Koenig's finger tightened for a full due. Then, freed he looked round dazed and shaky, to see the man crumpling to the floor.

Completely composed, Jarak said, 'As Commander here, you have a certain special value. It would be a needless waste to kill you before one of my people can make use of you. You must see your choice is between a future as one of us or no future at all.' Using the command console he made an announcement, 'Attention, all sections, Alpha. This is Jarak calling.'

His face appeared on every screen, mesmeric, compelling. As he continued to speak, the effect could be judged from the reaction in Main Mission. No eye could turn away. Power was being drained out of them. Men and women all over Moonbase Alpha began to collapse like puppets on a slackening string.

Jarak droned on, 'The mission of the spaceships over Alpha is nearly completed. My people are preparing now to transfer to those of your dying bodies which have been designated.'

At the communications post in the medicentre, all eyes were fixed on Jarak. Paula slipped unconscious to the floor. No one moved to help her. In Main Mission, Sandra Benes fell and Kano slumped across his desk. Koenig, gripping the edge of his command console saw Helena drop to her knees.

Inexorably, Jarak went on, 'When the transfer is complete, the space ships will lift off into space and self destruct. As far as our pursuer is concerned, we shall no longer exist. But we shall have begun our new life as inhabitants of Moonbase Alpha.'

Few heard him finish. Victor Bergman, arms sprawled across his desk was breathing in long shuddering gasps. Koenig, still hanging on to his desk felt consciousness ebbing away. He tried to concentrate on the green dome of the spacer he could dimly see through the direct vision ports of his command office. When it suddenly suffused with white flame, he believed his mind had finally blown.

Brilliant eye aching light flooded briefly through the complex. Rena, hand to her mouth turned in terror to Jarak. Her voice on a rising note of hysteria cut through the silent room, 'They've found us.'

Thuds on the outer skin of the dome told of debris cascading down from the shattered spacer. Jarak hesitated, saw Koenig pulling himself erect, took Rena's hand and ran with her into Main Mission.

Koenig hauled himself into his command chair, punched keys and saw the moon surface glow to life on the main scanner. Six new spacers in tight formation were arrowing in towards the moon. The three still in possession were leaving station, pulling away in a desperate bid to gain sea room.

There was a split in the racing squadron. Three fell away to come in from below. Jarak's force was moving into the jaws of a closing trap.

Koenig drew deep quivering breaths, feeling strength build again in his body. The staff in Main Mission were also stirring. Helena, Morrow, Carter were shakily on their feet. Kano was kneeling beside Sandra holding her hands. Of Jarak and Rena there was no sign.

He hit the Red Alert button and the strident klaxons sounded out. Picking a laser out of the pile, he rounded up Morrow and Carter and all the security men who were on their feet and led them after Jarak. This time he would make sure.

High above the complex, Jarak's leading spacer was hit by crossfire and disintegrated in white light. An attacker too keen and too close was shattered by a hail of debris and flared off in a wheeling arc of flame. It was a chance for the other two, who were through the gap and pulling away with the five remaining aggressors coming round to reform and pursue.

Helena Russell moved slowly into Main Mission. Medical instinct gave her bewildered mind a holdfast and she dropped wearily on her knees beside Sandra, loosened her tunic and smoothed her hair from her face. She reassured Kano. 'Don't worry. She's going to be all right.'

Now she could think it through, she was assessing their symptoms. Whatever Jarak had drummed up had struck at the central nervous system like a knock out blow to the diaphragm. Hopefully, now that the effect had stopped there would be no permanent damage. Feeling better by the minute, she looked around for Koenig and went on to find him.

Jarak and Rena, lasers set for a stun beam, were ahead of the posse. Racing along a connecting corridor, they bore down on a group of Alphans, who were dusting off and checking that they were still drawing living breath. A lithe girl, straightening her inner suit with a wiggle, saw them first and opened her mouth for a scream that never materialised. She was down again with the rest falling everywhichway.

There was one still on his feet who had nipped smartly behind the communications post, and Jarak and Rena, with perfect co-ordination, turned in as they ran past one either side and fired simultaneously. He fell like a tree.

They ran on, aiming for the medicentre as though Jarak had indentified that area as his home ground. At the door, Jarak used Koenig's commlock and they were through, Rena ran in like a commando, stun gun ready.

They were doing better than the hunted spacers. In the bitter dog fight across the stars, the five vengeful seekers had closed in. They were not having it easy. Working in concert, Jarak's two ships drove to break the net, firing tracers of green light at a single enemy. It disintegrated in a blinding flash and they were momentarily in the clear, separating to split the pack, one in a screaming climb, one dropping away.

The execution squad divided, two to each quarry. The lower one was a fraction slow and they were on it like stooping falcons, striking again and again until there was only a white void and the whole force could beat away after the single survivor.

On the ground, Jarak was using Koenig's commlock

to close the hatch of the medicentre while Rena had Mathias at gun point. Paula, taking longer to recover was still out, propped against pillows on a spare cot.

Jarak used the commlock to close the door, picked another channel and raised direct computer service. Mimicking Koenig's voice and transmitting a mental picture of Koenig's face to the screen he said, 'Computer?' waited a second for clearance and went on, 'Medicentre doors are to remain on lock until this direct command order is rescinded. Check?'

'Check, Commander.'

Satisfied, Jarak turned to Mathias, 'Now Doctor Mathias, I hope you will help me persuade your Commander to accept us as Alphans.'

Koenig's party fanned out round the medicentre door and Koenig, missing his commlock, called on Carter, 'Right Alan. Open it.' Carter's commlock buzzed and then blipped for non op. The door stayed shut. The commlock buzzed again and Kano's face appeared on the miniature screen, 'Alan, is the Commander with you?'

Koenig took it. 'Here Kano.' Kano looked worried, 'According to computer, you are inside the medicentre and have just issued a command that the door is to remain on lock.'

Morrow's commlock buzzed and Koenig checked the call over his shoulder. It was Jarak. Helena joined the group in time to hear him say, 'Commander Koenig?'

'Here.'

'We wish to negotiate.'

Helena cut in, 'He has Doctor Mathias and Paula.'

Koenig looked at her, made no comment, said evenly, 'Make your demands.'

Jarak's voice was conciliatory, 'Requests, Commander. We are no longer in a position to make demands.'

'Then it's simple. Open the door.'

'As a human, Commander, you are prey to emotion. Your heart is full of resentment at my treatment of Alpha's first mother and child.'

'Don't give me that, Jarak. You tried to kill us all.'

'It was to be a painless process of change. The combination of Alphan bodies and the minds of my people would have been splendid. The result would have ensured a great future for Alpha.'

'And us? Where would we be?'

'You would have become part of us. But we have failed. The rest of my people have been discovered and by now destroyed. Our request now is a modest one that we should become part of you.'

Not impressed, Koenig said, 'Jarak, you have just killed more of my people. You are holding two hostages.'

Jarak was almost pleading, 'Commander, once you chose to bargain with your own life. It is not our purpose to destroy. Your people are not dead.'

Helena Russell touched Koenig's arm, 'That is true. I checked. They are stunned only. They will recover.'

Jarak had gone silent and his face winced with pain as though he had received a sudden wound. Thousands of kilometres above his head the lone survivor of his fleet had taken its death knock, fighting to the last, but outgunned and out-manoeuvred by its four tormentors.

Jarak's face smoothed and he went on, 'We had become human and we translated our power and our threats into terms that human minds could understand. Now we are appealing to you as humans ourselves, appealing for your mercy.'

All eyes were on Koenig. It was a command decision that he could not pass on. It was a hard one. How could he not give them their chance? How could

41

he gamble with the very lives of his own people? The biological computer had more data than simple fact to sort through.

A commlock buzzed to break his concentration and Sandra was calling in from Main Mission, 'Commander, the spaceships are back.'

There was a pause as she watched them settle on the quadrants, taking up the positions that Jarak's force had held. Sandra said defeatedly, 'They have resumed their old stations and, Commander—' her voice notched up in agitation, 'the green lights are pulsating.'

Jarak's face on the commlock was running with sweat. He said hoarsely and with terrible finality, 'The people from our planet have found us, Commander. To destroy us they will destroy the whole of Alpha.'

The screen blanked as the commlock fell from his hand and Jarak took stumbling steps to meet Rena.

Green light was flooding in from every direct vision port, draining colour from every face, pulsing to a hypnotic flicker rhythm that held the Alphans still.

Mathias saw Jarak and Rena meet and cling, hungry and desperate for the comfort neither could give. He thought of Paula, turned to her and knelt by the bed, leaned over her as though to protect her with his body from the all pervading green light. How long he stayed there he never knew, but he sensed there was a change. The light had stopped. He could feel the movement of her diaphragm, she would be all right.

He pulled himself to his feet and looked around, checked even Cynthia Crawford's bed and then was back bewildered and doubting his sanity, trying to get through to Paula for another human opinion to tell him he was not mad.

Sandra Benes, putting the obvious on record, or convincing herself said, 'Commander, it has stopped and wait, I think yes,' excitement was choking her, 'they're leaving. The spaceships are leaving. They're pulling away.'

Koenig said urgently, 'Jarak?' There was no reply and he called again, 'Mathias?'

Nobody was answering. Switching his gun to laser beam, he sent a fine searing needle into the door panel to cut out the lock.

Carter and Paul Morrow forced back the door and Koenig went in at a run, laser ready to fire. Helena was close behind him and at first thought that Paula was dead and that Mathias was out of his mind with grief. She said sharply, 'Dr Mathias! Bob!'

But he was beyond rational speech, he could only point and she followed the direction.

Behind the screen, she met Cynthia Crawford's radiant eyes as she sat like any Madonna nursing her day-old child.

She called, 'John!' and he rounded the barrier ready for the next disaster.

It was unbelievable. It was true. It was a pay off that they had never expected to see. Something Jarak had said rose in Koenig's mind and he said slowly, 'Somehow, they must have made it good. They must have given themselves up to save the whole community.'

Koenig's commlock buzzed and as he flipped it open, Sandra's face, full of excitement appeared on the miniature screen. He had time to think, 'This is where we came in. Now they all go out of their heads over the baby.' But it was not Jackie Crawford that was lighting her lamp. She said, 'Commander. Please come to Main Mission. There's something you should see. I've alerted Professor Bergman.'

'What is it?'

'Long range probes are pulling something in. A small solar system. On this course we should pass close.'

CHAPTER THREE

It could be what they were looking for and it could be the run up to another disappointment. John Koenig wondered just how much his people could stand. But even Bergman was getting enthusiastic and only the biggest grouch of all time could not be moved by the optimism that was stirring through the base like an epidemic. Every spin of their hurrying moon brought confirmation. It looked good. It *had* to be good.

The scanner in Main Mission was showing a picture that outranked any Picasso. Lovingly tuned by Sandra Benes, there was a brilliant sun on a black velvet pad with a single satellite planet, rosy veined, shrouded in milk white cloud.

John Koenig studied the distant system from a direct vision port and turned to Bergman to see the astro chart he had drawn up. In plan, there was a simplicity and perfection about the system that clearly delighted the scientist. There was the sun with two planets on the same circular orbital path around it, balanced like balls on a governor in the piping days of steam.

At a tangent to the circle and running close to

the planet with the atmosphere shown on the scanner, Bergman had projected a tentative line of the course the Moon would take.

He said, 'It's incredible, John. A sun like ours, the planet Ariel with its atmosphere. It's a perfectly balanced little solar system.'

Koenig tapped the chart and tried to keep it rational, 'But if we go into orbit we'll offend your sense of symmetry, Victor.'

'If we go into orbit, I won't care about symmetry.'

'That will depend whether the planet lives up to Computer predictions. We should know soon enough. Alan should be getting close.'

He crossed to Sandra's desk and looked over her shoulder at the monitor. Alan Carter's leading Eagle was nudging into the upper limits of Ariel's atmosphere and the sound of rocket motors working in rarefied air was suddenly delivered strength nine. Carter's voice, sounding pleased, came up, 'Vapour trails. I'd almost forgotten how they looked.'

Sandra Benes put in a warning note, 'Eagle outer skin temperatures on the move. Going up fast!'

Beside her, Paul Morrow checked readings and spoke to Carter, 'Turn up the heat shields four points, Alan. Keep an eye on them.'

Over right, Helena Russell watched the sequence at her own desk. Making a subjective judgement, she said, 'This is not a computer analysis, but I'd say they were in a regular stratosphere.'

Koenig let the general euphoria wash over him. He knew what it meant to all personnel on Alpha. There were smiling faces all round Main Mission and Carter himself, seen in the distant Eagle was grinning like a boy. Falling into the mood, Koenig asked, 'How does it feel to be flying an airplane instead of a space shuttle, Alan?'

'It feels just great, Commander.'

Computer, joining in the exchange went into spasm and Kano tore off a read out and handed it to Bergman, 'Computer's flight plan for their planetfall.'

'No problems?'

'No problems.'

Bergman confirmed with a quick glance through and handed it on to Paul Morrow. 'Put it through to the on-board computer, Paul.'

It was going too well. Koenig's mind was probing ahead, trying to drum up snags they might have to meet. It was all too easy. The warning bleep on Carter's console, picked up by the repeater in Main Mission, jerked him out of his reverie.

Face suddenly serious, Sandra zoomed for a closer look and they picked it up as Carter's voice announced it. 'I have scanner contact. Alien object approaching.'

Out of the cloud layer below the Eagles, a bright sphere had surfaced like a mine bobbing to the surface of the sea. Then it was rising with increasing acceleration into full vision, round and brilliant with six projecting tubes in a frill.

Carter had it in direct vision, 'Visual contact. Alien object closing fast.'

They saw him bank steeply and turn off. But the sphere was throwing itself across the sky to stay dead ahead and cut the distance between them.

He tried again, throwing in every erg from the Eagle's screaming motors in a climb that pinned him back to his seat under mounting G. His voice was incredulous as he jerked out, 'It's homing on me. It's some kind of missile.'

Main Mission had gone quiet in a stunned silence. Carter, fighting it out to the last, was throwing the Eagle everywhichway with Johnson, the co-pilot and himself strained against their straps. It was not going to be any good. Johnson had his hands to his face in an instinctive gesture to protect himself as the sphere manoeuvred effortlessly to beat every avoiding ploy and closed in for the strike.

Cracked with effort, Carter's voice said 'I . . . can't . . . shake . . . it . . . off!' and his arm went up to shield his eyes from the blast.

There was not even the check of collision. When he slowly moved his arm to look out, he had gotten a bulbous end to the Eagle's nose cone. He was still staring at it, hardly daring to move, when Koenig's urgent voice cracked through the command cabin.

'Carter. Carter!'

Still moving slowly as though any sudden jolt might trigger the device, Carter said, 'We're still alive, Commander. It . . . it didn't detonate. It's just settled, soft as a puff ball.'

Main Mission was slow to react. As yet they had not had time to think of disappointment, another dream gone sour. They were simply bewildered by the suddenness of it. Koenig looked grimly along the line of faces, and leaned forward to speak into Sandra's intercom, 'Eagle Two and Eagle Seven— return to base.'

Then he spoke to Paul Morrow who seemed to have suddenly come alive and was staring at Sandra's classic profile as she looked at the scanner in bitter dismay.

'Paul. Evacuate personnel from launch pad One. Crash Unit stand by. Red Alert.'

Action broke the tension. All personnel moved to action stations. The promised land might have taken a knock, but they were professionals.

Koenig thought of the precept, 'Living is struggling. You'd better learn to like it.' Maybe that's what they were best at and a land flowing with milk and honey was not for them.

He watched the Eagles pull away and set a course for Alpha. He was still there monitoring every second of the mission as Carter brought Eagle Two in on a proving orbit with Eagle Seven keeping station.

Carter said, 'Approaching now for final descent.'

Koenig said, 'Pad one is sealed off. The moment your ship lands get the hell out of it. Skip procedures. Just aim to break records getting clear.'

Johnson and Carter exchanged glances. Carter said, 'Check, Commander. It hasn't stirred a hair so far.'

'My guess is it won't show its hand until you've brought it down.'

They watched him come in on the main scanner, until the Eagle was a bare metre off its pad. Paul Morrow took over control, delicately judging distances a centimetre at a time. A boarding tube snaked out urgently for the hatch and Carter and Johnson could be seen unclipping harness and making ready for a sprint start.

Release of tension could be felt all round the control desks as the two men whipped out of sight into the passenger module and a monitor flipped tell tales in a row to show its movement out.

Victor Bergman was a puzzled man. Nothing he could do was giving any information. Working from the Technical Work Shop, he was probing with remote X-Ray gear but he might as well have been using a pin hole camera.

A bleap sounded from the communications post and Koenig was back again asking questions. 'Victor, what are you getting?'

'Nothing, John. I can't get any readings at all.'

'Density? Radiation?'

'That object is totally resistant to any remote analysis technique we have.'

'Then we'll just *have* to bring it inside for you.'

When it was done and the sphere lay impassively on a work top, it reminded Koenig of an early Earth satellite, something meteorologists might have sent up. He said slowly, 'An intelligent civilisation, living in an atmosphere similar to Earth's, sees Earthmen coming and tries to prevent them. So by means of creating a diversion, it sets up a problem that it knows they will try to solve. And it works out. That's how we reacted. Does that make sense?'

Bergman said, 'It makes sense, but why should they do it?'

'To gain time? To find out more about us?'

Helena carried it one step further on, 'And to prevent us finding out anything about them?'

There was silence and they stood round the shining sphere. Alan Carter, anxious to try again said, 'I say let the Professor prod it about as much as he likes to keep it happy. But don't let's waste any more time before having another crack at the planet.'

Helena said, 'If we go into orbit round this sun, we'll have all the time we need.'

Optimism was rearing its head and Koenig said shortly, 'We don't know that.' It earned him a wide-eyed look from the medico, but he stuck to it, 'We don't know if we will go into orbit, any more than we know if this thing is friendly or hostile. But even if it turns out to be some kind of invitation card, we still have to play this step by step. What do you have this far, Victor?'

Bergman passed a hand over his wide forehead, 'Minimal information, I'm afraid. Weight at nineteen point two six kilogrammes: diameter one point two metres; temperature ambient; radiation zero. Composition still unknown.'

'Inert?'

'Totally.'

As if on cue, there was a percussive crack followed by a thin, high pitched whistle and six slender antennae extruded smartly from the bland surface of the globe.

It was an object lesson in not talking about any dumb creature before its face.

Koenig thought bitterly he should get himself analysed. He should never have had it brought inside. Helena was rooted to the spot and he took her by the shoulders pulling her away as the whistle notched itself up an octave into a scream. White vapour under immense pressure began to jet from a scatter of tiny opening valves.

Koenig yelled 'Gas' and signalled for out, fairly throwing Helena through the hatch. He saw Bergman and Carter out and backed out himself aiming his commlock to seal it off.

The hatch sliced shut, but immense pressure from inside was forcing thin jets of vapour from around the seals. Koenig said urgently, 'Helena. Medicentre. Prepare to receive casualties. Victor, get a sample. I want a run down on that gas sooner than possible.'

Before they were out of sight he was calling Morrow from the corridor communications post. 'Paul, Red Alert. Evacuate Technical Section at the double and seal off. Then open all its air locks to the surface.'

Klaxons sounded out, red lights flashed at all points in Moonbase Alpha in a man made frenzy. But as an alarm generator the sphere had the edge. Its frenetic scream was notched to a mind bending crescendo. Technicians scrambling out of their section in a state of shock, hardly knew whether they were moving from it or towards it. Gale winds tearing through the connecting corridors buffeted them and spun them about. Small trash lifted in cyclone eddies and slammed round in a confusing storm.

Watching from Main Mission, Koenig saw the last man out and Morrow, working with quick economical gestures flip through the sequences. Morrow's terse report 'Technical Area sealed off and ventilated,' came a split second after the monitors had already begun to show the effect.

Vapour and litter had made an instant course change, reacting to the vacuum suck of the moon surface. Roaring like a train, the gas was venting out through the air locks. A whirlwind billowed up the elevation shaft to launch pad one, spewing up a fountain of debris like a ticker tape welcome in reverse.

It looked like a spectacular death wound; as though Moonbase Alpha was emptying itself onto the moon's surface. Koenig asked, 'Does Computer have any assessment of the total capacity of that object?'

Kano had already asked it and had the answer pat, 'At present rate of expansion, Commander, no prediction. Which is to say, infinite.'

Paul Morrow put in, 'Pressure in the Technical Area was up by eighty before we could open the locks. It couldn't get out fast enough.'

It made no kind of sense, Koenig, thinking aloud, said, 'Diameter one point two, weight nineteen point two six. It just doesn't gell.'

Outside the escaping vapour had settled to a steady plume that ran like a column for half a kilometer and then billowed away in a spreading mist cloud. Through it there was a glint as though it had been shot with sequins and Tanya's urgent call brought Koenig round to a direct vision port. 'Commander, we're being invaded.'

Drifting down through the mist came an uncountable number of small spheres, identical with the one which had wrecked the interior of the Technical section. As they touched down, they began to stream with vapour. The moonscape had turned to geyser country.

Information was crowding Koenig. Bergman was calling urgently from the intercom, 'John! You'll never believe this. It's air. That thing has brought air.'

51

Tanya called him again, 'Commander. Only look at this!'

What she had to show was making its own impact in a flush of colour on every direct vision port and the desks emptied as all personnel in Main Mission crowded to the windows to look out.

Above the barren lunar surface the sky was flushing with a rose madder down. They had a bright sun like a warm penny standing on the horizon. They had sunlight breaking the harsh silhouettes of the ancient rocks. Moonbase Alpha was bathed in sunlight, spilling through the ports and lighting up every incredulous face.

Koenig looked higher. Above the rim of the horizon the sky was a clear wash of blue. Helena Russell and Victor Bergman came up beside him. He said, 'Red sunrise. Blue sky. There's an atmosphere. We have an atmosphere!'

They could only stare. Helena put a hand on his arm and they watched the sun jacking itself up above the horizon, bringing a day they had never expected to see.

Main Mission was in holiday mood and Koenig recognised what a difference it could make when the scene outside the windows was changed. Maybe he should have had them pasted over with travel posters from the beginning?

Sandra Benes hardly able to keep her voice steady reported to Morrow, 'Gravity's building, Paul. By the time we establish an orbit, it'll be near enough Earth equivalent to make no matter.'

It was all good news, bringing smiles all round. Their miracle was holding up.

Helena Russell came in, slim and tall, moving like a dancer, asking Kano, 'Has Computer processed my data?'

Before Kano could reply, it was in on the act, winking a green light and presenting a read-out for Kano to hand over. It needed only a glance. She said, 'Computer's telling us nice stories today.' Then she went on, knowing what he was going to say and making a nicely timed duet of it, 'Computer never tells stories.'

She took the slip to Koenig, 'I can only test for elements we know and can identify. There *may* be other ingredients that our instruments don't register.'

It was a pleasure to look at her at any time but when she was happy, there was a radiance about her which he would not have traded for any Mediterranean Sun. He had to make himself put the hard question, 'What about ultra-violet? That was your main concern.'

'Above twenty thousand, the atmosphere begins to thin off rapidly. On Earth that would be hardly thick enough to act as a filter. But here? Well, I can only say I think we're going to be all right.'

'But the final test is to breathe it.'

'And *live* in it.'

Koenig considered it. First reaction was to take her by the hand and lead her out into the sunlight, but there was procedure and he went by the book, standing up and walking out to the steps above Main Mission.

He spoke to them all. 'Doctor Russell is satisfied that, as far as she can judge from processed data, this atmosphere is breathable and safe. All we need now is two volunteers to make sure.'

It was a sell out as he had expected. All personnel in Main Mission were voting with their feet—here I am, send me. Paul Morrow and Sandra had the edge. They had already been standing, deep in a personal conversation and caught Koenig's eye. He said, 'Very well. It's Paul and Sandra. But let's be clear.

This is the pay off in a scientific investigation not a joy ride. Mind you, I think, Kano, along with the other checks you should monitor joy level for the album.'

It was a popular choice. In the shifting pattern of relationships on Alpha, Morrow and Sandra were circling each other for a hold. Whether they knew themselves it was so or not, the onlookers, ahead of the game, had sensed it and there was a clap from all hands when they left to dress for the outing as though they were to be the first pair for a new Garden of Eden.

Tanya monitored them into the lock and threw the picture on the main scanner as a production number. Sealed up, with helmets closed, they could be seen waiting for the green light.

Paul Morrow's voice trying to keep factual, asked for clearance, 'Confirm air lock pressure equalised with atmosphere?'

Helena said steadily, 'Confirmed, Paul. You're clear to move out now.'

A green tell tale glowed over the hatch and Morrow directed his commlock at the panel. They stepped out hand in hand, bulky incongruous figures to be bathed in brilliant sunshine. Ten paces from the lock, they stopped. Morrow lifted a bulky thumb and then patted Sandra's dome. Standing apart each made gradual adjustments to external valves.

Still monitoring, Helena Russell said, 'You're breathing more air than oxygen now. Pressures inside and outside your suits are equal. How does it feel?'

Morrow said, 'I feel fine,' and looked at Sandra.

Trying to be objective, she said, 'My pulse rate's increasing.'

It got a laugh from all hands in Main Mission. Helena had already noticed it, 'I'm monitoring that. Put it down to simple excitement. Outside temperature, rock steady at twenty-four Celsius.'

Morrow had his gloves off and was wiggling his fingers giving them a treat in natural sunshine. Sandra unsealed her gauntlets, drew them off and dropped them at her feet. She stood still watching Morrow with eyes enormous, as he joined her and flipped her helmet release catches. Before lifting off her visor, he unsealed his own, drew it off and sniffed the air cautiously like an animal waking after hibernation. Reassured, he said, 'Smells good!'

Helena who had reckoned air was air and should be neutral said quickly, 'Like what?'

'Like fresh country air. Just what the doctor ordered!'

Sandra could wait no longer. Opening her visor, she inhaled for a long count, held it and breathed out, looking pink and radiant. They had forgotten Main Mission and moved instinctively together, tangling bulky harness and only managing a light brushing kiss. But it was a first in Eden and drew a spontaneous cheer.

The Alphan days were not long enough. They were turning Moonbase Alpha into a Lido and everybody was ready to work round the clock. Koenig and Helena and Victor Bergman watched two technicians put the finishing touches on a regular glazed window for the Technical Section. Simple things still gave pleasure and as the men picked up their gear, Helena opened it and looked out with a warm breeze ruffling her hair.

Groups of Alphans were lying about on cushions, under improvised gay awnings. Alan Carter and Tanya had a badminton game under way. There was a festive air about.

She said, 'Now we have to worry about not sitting in a draught.'

Koenig said, 'So we've traded one set of problems for another.'

A tannoy blared out and the lotus eaters turned lazily to listen to the next ration of good news, 'Today's sun session has been extended by ten minutes due to generally increased levels of tolerance to radiation throughout the spectrum. Individuals with lower than average tolerance ratings will be reminded via their medical monitors when their time has expired.'

Koenig leaned both hands on the low table where the first satellite still remained. In spite of the normality outside, the bursts of laughter and Alan Carter calling the score to Tanya, he could not be at ease. He said, 'I get the feeling it's here to watch us. The rest of them pulled out as soon as they'd built up the atmosphere. Why not this one? What's it doing here?'

Victor Bergman tapped it with a stylus. 'I've tried Spectro-X. I've tried radio analysis. I've even tried cutting into it with a laser. No dice. Nothing gives.'

Defending it, Helena said, 'In our ignorance we've suspected it of all kinds of malice, but so far, it's been the biggest benefactor we've had in space.'

Koenig said quietly, 'I know Victor is worried that things are not as rosy as they seem.'

'In what way?'

Bergman looked at her, choosing his words carefully, 'We're not in orbit yet around this sun and I'm not sure we're going to be.'

The implications needed no spelling out. Helena returned to the new window and looked at the sun lovers, 'I don't like to think what would happen if they realised it was only an interlude.'

Koenig joined her, spoke close to her ear, moved by the smell of sun on her hair, 'We'd have to accept it. Just as we had to accept that we'd never see Earth again.'

In the distance, Paul Morrow and Sandra were

walking hand in hand towards the low range of moonrock that marked the perimeter. Somebody wolf whistled. A few short days had brought a normality that looked fixed for all time.

Bergman said, 'I'm having a little trouble calculating seasonal predictions. But instinct seems to say this is Spring.'

He would have been more sure on the count, if he could have monitored Paul and Sandra round the convoluted twist which screened them from the *hoi polloi*.

Stretched on a smooth slab, they looked across the familiar moon desert. Sandra said, 'No sensors, no monitors, no computers. We must have done the longest duty tour on record. We deserve a break.'

'We have one. But it isn't exactly a home from home.'

'Anything to be out of Alpha.'

'It puts things in a new light.'

'Sunlight!'

'Seriously though. It's more than that. If this is the end of one life, we have to start to build a new one. One where we can live like human beings again.' He picked out a loose rock and pitched it at a dusty tump. It was still a novelty to hear sounds on the moon surface.

Sandra said, 'Do you know what sounds I've come to miss most?'

'Birdsong?'

'Children playing. All the nonsense things they get up to.' She was watching him, head turned in the crook of her arm, eyes questioning. There was a sense that they had all the time in the world in front of them and he was very still, feeling the electric tension between them like a charge of static.

Hardly more than breathing it, he said, 'Cooped up in Alpha, there are thoughts we can't allow ourselves to have. Here we are free to speak what we feel. Sandra?'

Her eyes were wide, almost all pupil and gently affirmative. Skin was sun warmed, smooth as alabaster, mouth an open O, soft and dissolving.

It was a homecoming that the moon's ancient rocks had never expected to see.

In practical terms, homecoming was Bergman's theme in the command office as he spread a large scale lunar map on the conference table. He said, 'Here, right here. This old Moon could become new Earth. We could settle and build outside Alpha. Fertilise the lunar dust. Raise crops.'

Koenig said, 'All we need is rainfall.'

'We can make that, the air's rotten with humidity. All we do is start the cycle, sow the clouds with crystals.'

'Not so fast, Victor. It took twenty-five years to reclaim the Sahara.' He pointed out through the window, 'But out there is a planet that already supports some kind of civilisation. Our priority must be to find out if it can or will support us.'

In Main Mission, monitor equipment keeping tabs on Bergman's mystery sphere was reporting activity to an empty desk. The frill of antennae was creeping out. There was a pause at full extension and then eye-searing light streaked out from the shining tips, flaring away in a zig zag to the heavily clouded sky.

Paul Morrow and Sandra heard it on their rock as a thunder crack and could not tell whether it was a phenomenon from the external world or a mental event. It took a repeat to have them sitting up staring towards Alpha.

Koenig and Bergman raced for a window to see forked lightning run along the underside of the clouds. There was a patter of large drops of rain, warm as blood and a scatter of sun bathers to get inside. Then the rain flurry was a deluge and they were out again, capering like crazy children in the first rain they had seen for too long.

Paul Morrow was holding Sandra in the rain, her hair flattened in a sheath, water running over her shoulders, falling from the points of her breasts like a nymph in a fountain. They ran hand in hand through the rain to join the crowd on the forecourt.

Alan Carter shouted to them, 'Tomorrow we'll build a pool.'

It was good thinking, but Paul Morrow was a committed man. He said, 'Tomorrow we build the New Alpha.'

In the command office, Bergman could not keep still. Vindicated on his main point, he was letting imagination take over, 'You see, the cycle has already begun. The Sea of Tranquillity will become a genuine sea. Craters will fill and become beautiful circular lakes. John, we have a beautiful new world!'

'How long will it take?'

'How hard will it rain?'

'Your circular lakes will look wonderful. But at the bottom of one of your craters, Victor, will be Moonbase Alpha like a surrealist folly.'

There was no doubt that the mood on Moonbase Alpha was to start building and Koenig bowed to it. Planet Ariel could wait for investigation. They would have their own small world and go calling on neighbours when their own city was rising from the ancient moon dust.

He had Carter set up an Eagle as a research module, stacked with equipment, seismographs, food, medical supplies, gas cylinders. He chose a small team. Carter himself as the most experienced pilot, Paul and Sandra, to give them something else to think about and Helena as a cool head.

Briefing them in Main Mission, he made it formal for all to hear. 'The expedition will be under the overall command of Doctor Russell. It's a straightforward brief. We have searched the Universe for another Earth and now, thanks to the mysterious people of Planet Ariel, we have found it right in our own back yard. Your job is to find the best site for us to begin our new future. Good luck to you all.'

The morning shift of sun bathers waved them off as Carter with Morrow beside him in the co-pilot slot gunned the loaded Eagle and lifted it from the pad. He circled once; treated all hands to a victory roll and arrowed off.

Inside Main Mission, Kano had Morrow's executive desk and controlled the flight. Meticulously on schedule, Carter called in, 'Eagle Two Eight reporting from the Crater Sea.'

'Check. We're watching you, Alan.'

Bergman was still drooling over his map, 'Two great rivers could flow together at this point. Great civilisations have always started in river valleys. The ideal site for a great commercial city would be. . . .'

He had lost Koenig's attention and stopped. Koenig said, 'Sorry, Victor. I hope we're not wasting our time. Suppose we don't make the orbit? We lose this sun. This atmosphere will be a liability, it will freeze. We shall be living in an ice field.'

'It's a calculated risk and we calculated it.'

'Other problems may come up. It may be too late to go to Planet Ariel.'

'You should have gone on the expedition, John. Something positive for you to think about.'

'Maybe you're right. I just hate waiting for answers.'

In the Eagle, Carter was flying low towards massed

cloud. Paul Morrow said, 'Thick cumulous rain cloud forming over the Taurus mountains.'

Carter said, 'Not much evidence of rainfall down below.'

'What do you expect, instant green fields?'

He called through to the passenger module, 'How are you feeling back there?'

Sandra answered, 'For me—air sick. That's why I chose the space programme!'

Helena Russell was having equipment trouble, 'This data transmitter's beginning to sound like a primitive crystal set.'

The same problem was troubling Kano. He reported, 'Computer can't read much of this data. There's too much interference.'

Defensively, Tanya who was filling in for Sandra, said, 'I have all the filters in. It's the best I can get.'

'They must be approaching an electric storm. An atmosphere is a mixed blessing.'

Koenig moved to the vacant seat beside him, 'I heard that. Not to me it isn't.'

'Communications are bad, Commander—back to the crackle and static of Earth.'

'Keep them plotted. If you look like losing them, abort the mission.'

Carter was enjoying himself. Meeting the outriders of the storm he was using skills that had not been called on in space missions. He said, 'Now this is really flying!'

His enthusiasm was not shared, Morrow saw the billowing hammerhead of a cumulo-nimbus and for his money it looked like a disaster. In the passenger module, Sandra and Helena were having a running fight with shifting cargo as the Eagle was thrown about.

Even Carter was finding that he now had to struggle to keep his Eagle airborne. He called control.

'Hello Alpha. This is Eagle Two Eight. Severe turbulence on the run up to the Taurus Mountains. I'm going over the top.'

A jag of lightning flicked past the undercarriage. There was no response from Alpha and he tried again, 'Hello Alpha. Hello Alpha. I'm not receiving you.'

There was no joy. In Main Mission, Koenig was on the same tack. 'Eagle Two Eight. We are not receiving you. If you hear me, abort. This is an order. Return to base.'

He handed over to Tanya, 'Keep trying.'

As she took over, saying again and again, 'Eagle Two Eight. Come in Eagle Two Eight . . . ,' he spoke to Kano, 'Compute their position, exactly.'

Eagle Two Eight was putting on a display of virtuoso aerobatics that would have stolen a show. Flung around in violent updraughts, she was more often on her back than on an even keel. Carter was suddenly fighting for their lives and knew it. He called urgently to Morrow for more power, 'We're losing power. Main boosters.'

Morrow flipped a lever. There was no response. He said, 'Malfunction. No main booster.'

'Back up power!'

Morrow tried again, said bitterly, 'Malfunction. No back up.'

Carter was looking incredulously at his console, 'All systems out. Crash positions.'

Behind their backs, the air lock hatch sliced shut with a definitive click.

The Eagle was falling like a rock, plummeting down out of cloud cover into a swirling vortex of moon dust. Fighting to the last centimetre, Carter had partially levelled off as it made its landfall, grinding into a brand new dust dune like a mad mole, burying itself, with the dust storm building a drift around it, turning it into a bland feature of the dune itself.

CHAPTER FOUR

Tanya went right on calling, though with everybody else in Main Mission, she had given up any rational hope of getting an answer.

'Come in Eagle Two Eight. Do you copy? Eagle Two Eight. Come in Eagle Two Eight . . .'

Koenig said, 'Kano, I want every Eagle fuelled and ready for take-off. I want photographs. Every square centimetre on a five hundred kilometre radius of their last position.'

Bergman was at his elbow and got the next chore, 'Look at it, Victor, make a plan of search. Twenty-seven zones.' Without waiting for agreement, Koenig raised the medicentre and tapped impatiently until Bob Mathias appeared on the screen.

'Mathias?'

'Commander?'

'Load medical supplies and rescue gear into Eagle One. You're coming with me.' Thinking aloud as much as speaking to Bergman, he went on, 'To lose all contact at less than ten thousand kilometres. In this century! It just isn't possible.'

Bergman said, 'We've had to come to terms with space. In the process we've simply forgotten the hazards of normal atmosphere.'

Shocked out of holiday mood, the personnel of Moonbase Alpha heaved round with a will. Out of a seeming chaos, serviced Eagles rose to the launch pads and took off in a steady stream, heading out low over the lunar surface.

The storm had died away as quickly as it began. Eagle Two Eight was a camouflage job, buried in its drift with a couple of metres of girderwork and a cocked up tail pipe to mark its tomb.

The wall of cargo containers and technical gear stored behind the seats in the passenger module had broken loose and turned itself into a knee deep scatter of trash. Food spilled out of shattered containers and spoiled in the baking heat, water seeped from fractured tanks, moondust leaked in like sand in an hour glass.

Sandra had taken the biggest beating and was still out, dodgily balanced over the debris on the one serviceable stretcher. While Paul Morrow and Helena set it up and made her comfortable, Carter was stripped to the waist, glistening with sweat as he ripped panel after panel from the bulkheads to lay bare blackened and smoking circuitry.

Wiping his forehead with his arm, he looked round the wreck, 'It's every transistor. Every last bleeding condenser. There isn't one not blown.'

Helena Russell said, 'The lightning. It must have burned out every circuit. We are dependent on Alpha to find us.' Even as she said it, she recognised the command responsibility and knew that as a plain fact it was no boost to morale. Paul Morrow's face across the bier confirmed it. She was on Koenig's home ground and she wished he was at hand. But as a working principle, she could see Morrow would be better on load.

'Paul, give Alan a hand. Get air in here.'

He hardly heard, taking Sandra's limp hand, he was looking at her face as though he could force a reaction by an effort of will. Helena said again, 'Don't worry. She's going to be all right.'

Dr. Helena Russell announces the birth of the first child ever born in space: "It's a boy. Mother and baby doing just fine. And little Jackie Crawford, Jr. is just beautiful!"

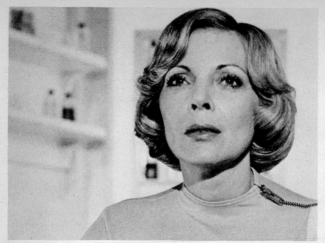

Dr. Russell is horrified: "In normal terms, Commander, young Jackie is physically about five years old—and it's happened in a matter of seconds!"

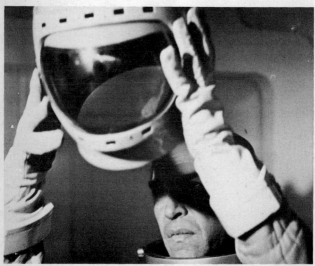

The green lights of four alien ships hover ominously over Moonbase Alpha—and John Koenig will go out on foot to challenge them.

The astronaut's heart pumps furiously, but action clears his head as he steps into the dark unknown. He is an anonymous but deadly figure in full space gear.

Moonbase Alpha's last resort is a small landing party of men armed with lasers, ready to engage alien forces in ruthless hand-to-hand combat.

Koenig and Bergman stare in disbelief. In little Jackie Crawford's place stands a grown man with fair hair and piercing eyes.

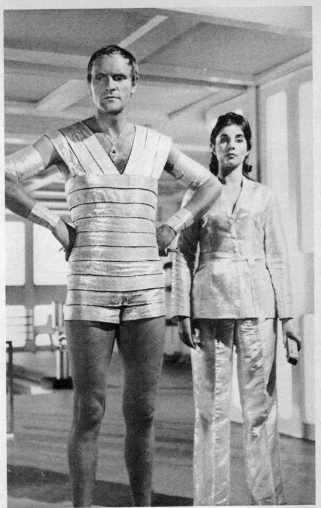

"My name is Jarak. The people of my planet have found us. To destroy us, they will destroy the whole of Alpha."

Loose gear crashes and the crew, caught unaware, tumbles toward the deck. Blackness folds on blackness, creating a unique instant—the moment of creation all over again!

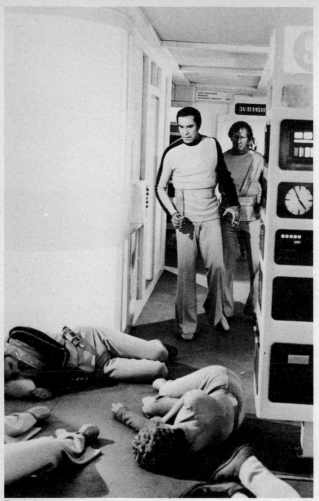

Red Alert blasts through the narrow corridors. Laser drawn, John Koenig chases Jarak, vowing that no more Alphans will die.

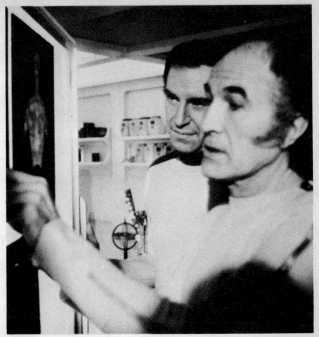

Koenig gasps when Professor Bergman shows him the medical department's report. It is impossible, but the scan shows that the patient has two brains!

Somehow the runaway moon accelerates, blasting the crew of Alpha into uncharted dimensions of the galaxy. They are traveling faster than the speed of light.

They brush the dust from the dead astronaut's visor, half expecting to see something horrible. But the reality is too much to stand—they recognize the distorted face beneath the mask!

"Our tools, our technology, our intellects—these are our future," Professor Bergman tells Commander Koenig. "As our situation improves, so will our chances for survival."

Commander Koenig watches in confusion as the strange Bergman calmly arranges plants. "This is another world, another time, another place," Koenig thinks. "It is a unique instant I was never meant to see."

The Earth people had forged their settlement out of sheer rock, building domes for their shelters and coaxing plants out of the hard ground. But there is no warmth or friendliness here.

They had attacked like a hostile tribe defending their territory. "Go back!" they had said. "We've fought hard for our lives here and you won't destroy them."

Alan Carter said, 'There are twenty-seven service-able Eagles available for a search plan. A pound to a pinch of porridge not one of them's still on the pad.'

Morrow stood up. It was all true. They were alive and that couldn't be bad. Without a word, he joined Carter and began to hurl debris away from the main hatch.

Almost directly overhead, Koenig was turning his Eagle.

Mathias in the co-pilot seat said, 'Right on the co-ordinates for the last radar contact, Commander.'

Leaving a vapour trail, Koenig made a long sweep, the moonscape was showing no trace. It was still not much of a New World and still the last place to be lost in.

Carter and Morrow had the hatch cleared to open, but the quick release gear had jammed solid. Morrow, streaked with sweat and dust wrenched out a seat rail and shoved it home in the manual locking union. As he threw his weight against it, there was a sharp crack and the weakened hatch burst inboard followed by a sliding wall of choking dust.

Grey clouds billowed around the module and Helena tore off her tunic to make a cowl over Sandra's face.

Morrow, struggling thigh deep, hauled himself across to check that she was all right and then waded back to where Carter had hauled himself out onto the dune. There was a saucer depression where the moondust had fallen inside, but otherwise the Eagle was melding into cover.

Paul Morrow said, 'Some camouflage job.' But Carter had spotted the dying line of Koenig's vapour trail and was going along the crest in a stumbling run, shouting, 'We're here. We're here. Come back, you morons!'

As they watched, the vapour trail faded over the horizon. Morrow said, 'We came to choose a site for the New Alpha. Looks like it has to be here.'

Certainly there were no contenders. They had moondust, a burrow and an achingly empty sky.

Grim faced, Koenig checked in at Main Mission. The hours of searching had made it clear enough that only blind chance was going to bring Eagle Two Eight to light. He leaned heavily on the back of Kano's chair, 'News?'

Kano shook his head, 'They've run out of daylight, Commander. The last Eagle's coming in.'

'Have them refuelled immediately.'

He went through into the command office where Bergman was poring over a chart. Doing his best to find something good in the day, Bergman said, 'It's looking promising, John. The moon is still curving in nicely towards an orbital path. Gravitational forces will continue to increase. The high point's due in eight days.'

Koenig was in no mood for comfort. He had looked at moondust until his eyes ached and he was seeing Helena Russell somewhere down there. He said harshly, 'The margins are too small. Our chances of going into orbit are no better than fifty-fifty. Right?"

On a direct question, the scientist had to nudge aside the optimist. Bergman spread his hands.

Koeing went on, 'So. If we don't make the orbit, conditions on the surface will deteriorate. And so fast that I don't like to think about it. Where does that leave them?'

Working like maniacs, Carter and Morrow had brought some order into the wrecked interior but they had more to consider than judging odds on the orbit. Vital supplies seemed to have taken a selective knock. When Helena picked out the last container and found it vile smelling and penetrated by acid, it was the last straw for Carter, who was feeling guilty anyway about the crash.

Helena said, 'Briassic acid. It smashed right through the life support systems.'

He wheeled round from the hatch, which he was trying to fix, looking angry. 'Why was it allowed anywhere near the food?'

'It wasn't. It arrived in the stores section along with the main motor. We're just lucky it didn't explode right then.'

'Maybe.'

'Come on Alan,' she took his arm and guided him into the command module hatch away from Sandra's hearing, 'Ease up a little will you? We have survival rations.'

Heavily sarcastic he said, 'Oh sure! About a half pint of drinkable water. That's great! It's only sixty Celsius in the shade. What's that going to do for Sandra with fractured ribs and a rising fever? She needs all the water she can get.'

Paul Morrow, squatting beside the stretcher heard it and waited for Helena's reply. Still keeping it cool, she said, 'All right. Then you make sure the next time they fly over, they can see us.'

Morrow was on his feet in a new burst of energy, 'Let's get some of this junk out of here. We have to lay out some kind of marker.'

They worked at it for an hour, humping containers out into the dust and hauling them in a line. The wind, which had dropped away was notching up again raising small spirals and driving tiny abrasive particles into their eyes and caking on their sweating skin. They had a half formed cross, but already the dust storm was blurring the outline with new drifts. Even Morrow conceded they had to stop. They crawled back into the dusty womb of the Eagle and sat speechless watching Helena, a doctor without a back-up service fall back to wiping her patient's face with a tattered rag.

Riding the storm, on continuous mission, Koenig was not far off in a geographical sense, but he knew for a truth he might as well be back at his desk in Moonbase Alpha. Only high points of rock showed through the swirling dust. It was confirmed when he looked at Mathias's face. They were wasting their time. Without a word, he made the course change and headed back, face set in a mix of despair and anger.

Helena Russell set out four beakers on a crate lid. It was colder and she had pulled on a space suit to conserve body heat. Moving clumsily, she opened a phial and dropped a tablet in each cup.

Alan Carter, cross legged, was flapping his arms to keep warm. Morrow took Sandra's hand and put it to his cheek. He said, 'She'll die out here.' It was unanswerable and Helena did not try. He went on, 'Sixty Celsius all day and freezing at night. What chance does that give her?'

Carter stood up, fished a space suit out of the ruck and began to climb into it. He said abrasively, 'You were the one. You rooted pretty hard for this crazy scheme of settling out here, instead of going down to the planet.' He leaned towards Morrow as though accusing him of standing in the way, 'I have this theory that down on Ariel the women are something fantastic.'

Reacting to the tone, Morrow said deliberately, 'No one could reckon on a so-called top pilot flying into a cloud bank for kicks.'

Helena moved between them, 'Let's save all the aggression for the fight we've already got for survival.' She measured water into the beakers and Morrow watching the level fall in the transparent container said, 'Make it three.'

Carter looked at him and then at Sandra. 'That's right. I'll go halves with Paul.'

Helena took a firm line, 'Sandra won't survive unless *we* do. Take your ration.' Without waiting for an argument, she handed them each a cup. There was silence as they sipped it like some rare wine and Morrow touched Sandra's hair. 'There must be something we can do.'

'Sure,' Carter was still troubled by black bile, 'we'll just walk.'

He would have been more angry if he could have heard Kano's report to the command office. Bergman and Koenig had a spread of air photographs and were doing a detailed search. Kano, knowing a messenger of gloom is never welcome for himself, said diffidently, 'Eagle One Five is grounded, Commander.'

He was right to be cautious, Koenig's snarl was full of menace, 'Grounded?'

'Apparent seizure of the lateral stabilisers. So far five Eagles have reported similar faults.'

Koenig's shout had every head in Main Mission looking up towards the office. 'We can't afford faults! We spend months drifting in space and the Techs have no better thing to do than sit on their fat asses. Now, when we need every Eagle we can get, you say they have faults? No Eagle goes off search until I say. Tell those lousy Techs to get their fingers out!'

Nobody had seen him so angry. Kano backed off, said quietly, 'Check, Commander.'

Bergman tried reason, 'They're breaking their necks in the Technical Section, John.'

'So they should.'

'Look, John, I hate to say this but you should face the possibility that we might not find them at all.'

It earned him a hard, angry stare and Koenig scattered the photographs, stood up and made for the hatch, 'I'll find them, Victor. I'll find them.'

Picking up Mathias on the way, he slammed out to the pad and climbed into Eagle One, lifting it in a howl of acceleration.

Chancing his arm, Kano called from Main Mission, 'Nice lift off, Commander. No systems malfunction indicated.'

Mathias scanning the co-pilot console was giving a thumbs up signal and Koenig answered control, 'No problems here, Kano. I'm clearing Alpha on two four zero.'

Fractionally late, Victor Bergman, carrying a component from a grounded Eagle, called 'Stop him, Kano! Bring him in.'

As if on cue, the auto crash alarm sounded out and they could see the nose of Eagle One take a dip. Koenig was getting no response from any control. He fairly spat into the communicator, 'Doesn't anything work any longer on this base?'

The Eagle was down, straddling the crater rim in swirling dust and Koenig was thumping the instrument spread with a balled fist, 'Well?'

Bergman answered, 'Something in the atmosphere, coupled with incessant flying in fine dust. Together they've added up to a rapid corrosive effect. Your control systems simply seized.'

Koenig's anger suddenly evaporated as he saw a new angle. 'Something in the atmosphere? We've got that atmosphere now in every section of Alpha.'

'Inside, the corrosion would be slower.'

He had lost his listener, Koenig was calling Kano.

'Yes, Commander?'

'I want windows replaced in every section of Alpha. Every air lock resealed. Re-pressurisation with our own atmosphere is to start as of now. Get to it.' Before

Kano could answer, he was back to Bergman, 'You say *every* Eagle has this?'

'Check. But there's one hopeful feature. Parts covered with that new graphite compound have escaped it. They have immunity to this corrosion.'

'How long to strip down one Eagle and graphite every exposed surface?'

Bergman was glad to be able to say, 'I have them started on it—technical estimate—three days.'

'Make that two days and, Victor, that satellite, get it outside the section. Dump it on the surface.'

For the record, it was night in the passenger module of Eagle Two Eight but it could have been any time in a mind numbing cycle of pain and exhaustion. Sandra Benes moaned, checked it, biting her lips, opened her eyes. Morrow raised himself on one elbow, leaned over, touched her forehead.

The contact calmed her, she even managed a smile. 'Paul?'

'You're getting better. You're going to be all right.'

He reached for one of the beakers and held it for her while she drank. Gaining a little strength, she tried to sit up, but very gently, he restrained her.

'I thought we'd found our new home.'

'We have. Never doubt it. We have.'

'But . . .'

'Don't try to talk, I'll get you another drink.'

He drained the last from the container and supported her while she drank deeply. Then she looked at the cup sensing something different. 'Has it rained?'

'Yes. Drink up. It has rained.'

She lay back, suddenly cold in spite of the wraps they had found for her. Her eyes closed. Morrow stood up slowly, stripped off his space suit and added it to the pile. The movement disturbed her and she was awake again, 'Paul?'

He put his finger to his lips in a mime for quiet, picked up the empty container and pointed to the hatch. She smiled vaguely as though she hardly understood, but whatever he did was A-Okay in her book.

As the hatch opened, wind and dust jetted in. He turned to look at her again and she lifted a hand to wave. Then he was through and the hatched closed.

Sensing something unusual, Helena Russell woke suddenly and saw Sandra looking across at her. She sat up aching in every limb and noticed Morrow's empty berth.

'Sandra? Where's Paul?'

'Gone to fetch water.'

Helena pulled herself to her feet and struggled with the hatch, blown dust needled her skin as she looked out into swirling darkness.

She called twice, 'Paul? Paul?' But there was only the everlasting moan of the wind to answer. There was nothing she could do and she set her back to the hatch to heave it shut.

Sandra, out of reach of reason, was suddenly enthusiastic, 'Paul said it rained again.'

'Did he? Oh, yes . . .'

'Was it a heavy fall?'

'Oh, not a lot. More a promise of things to come, really.'

Outside, Paul Morrow was moving in random circles. He looked at the water carrier in his hand and pitched it away into darkness. Stumbling on, he reached a rock outcrop, turned and set his back to it. Then allowed himself to slide down. It was the butt and seamark of his utmost sail. It would serve as a headstone as well as the next thing. As his hands reached ground level they were digging into something soft and moist as moss and he brought a handful up to his eyes. It was white, mushroom like in texture. He smelled it. It seemed wholesome. Squeezing it, he had drops of moisture running on the back of his hand and he licked them off. He pushed a piece in his dry mouth and began to chew.

Strength and resolution were flooding back like a tide. The wind dropped, dust settled. He had a minimum of light to work by. Slowly at first and then gathering momentum, he began to shift the scattered empty containers and build them round as the foundation footings of a hut. When Carter joined him at first light, he was up to shoulder level and between them they ripped out lengths of cladding for a pitched roof. It was a Heath Robinson structure at best, but Morrow was inordinately proud of it, as though he was seeing it as a Winter Palace.

Helena was dubious about it as any improvement on what they had but she could not withstand Morrow's new found enthusiasm. In any event, it was activity and a boost to morale. She helped fix a bed for Sandra and made no objection when he went to carry her out.

Sandra was conscious, though very weak and asked, 'Where are you taking me?'

'Home. The new city of Alpha.'

Whether she saw it as it was or whether some mental link helped her to share his vision, she made no comment.

He carried her over his threshold, saying, 'At least we've made a start. You'll be cooler here when the sun gets up. Not cooped away in that rat hole out of the air.'

'Thank you, Paul.'

He kissed her gently and set her down. 'We have found our new home. We just have to make the best of it. We're the first New Earthmen. This is the Garden of Eden.'

'It's a lovely thought, Paul. To begin the saga of the human race all over again.'

Helena and Carter had tactfully given them a time alone and finally came in. Morrow had another surprise. On a clean sheet of plexiglass, he had dumped a mound of his white mushroom material and quickly split it into four portions.

He said simply, 'Breakfast?'

Helena said, 'What is it, Paul?'

'Manna, if you like. Food from heaven. Or maybe from the people of planet Ariel, if you prefer.'

'Wait a minute. Where has it come from?'

'It's growing. Out there under the rocks. Like mushrooms.'

'We have no means of analysing it, running a test. We can't eat it until we know the composition.'

Paul Morrow was impatient, 'You have your test. *I've* eaten it.'

Helena looked at him closely, noticing the febrile glitter in his eyes and his quicker, nervous movements. 'You've eaten it?'

He nodded, looking insanely pleased with himself and she flared angrily, 'Sandra?'

'Not yet. I was waiting until we were all together.' He stood by Sandra defensively and went on, 'The change in Sandra's condition is born of hope. But man does not live on hope alone.'

He took a portion of the mushroom growth and knelt beside the bed. Helena was quick to intercept and took it from his hand before Sandra could open her mouth. She said, 'Paul, you must see we have to take care.'

Carter was suddenly in Morrow's corner, 'It doesn't seem to have done him any harm. He put most of this together single handed. He's got the strength from somewhere.'

At the same time, Paul Morrow seemed to have found a persuasive tongue, 'The way I see it, this is no accident. The moment I lie down to die, this stuff appears literally at my side. Be reasonable. They could be months finding us here. Every time we clear a signal area on the ground, dust drifts over it. Maybe we'll never see another Eagle. Yesterday we had no hope. Let's not kid ourselves. We were in a terminal situation. Today we have hope and something to sustain it.'

Carter at least was a convinced man, 'I say don't knock it, Doc.'

Morrow restated the brutal fact. 'We have no alternative. We either eat it or die.'

Medical training fought a rearguard. Reluctantly, Helena Russell said, 'All right. But I insist we stick to the ration while I do what tests I can. If I can't find any positive harm and Paul is still okay, then I'll give it clearance.'

Morrow was disappointed. 'How long will you take?'

'Will you give me to midday?'

She got a grudging nod. Carter said, 'Just in case it's okay, I'm going mushrooming.'

John Koenig was becoming a solitary. Staff in Main Mission drew lots to take any message into the command office where he was keeping a vigil like a captain in a homebound clipper driving his ship in a half gale.

Even Victor Bergman came in with reservations. Carrying a restricted read-out from Computer, he found Koenig at a direct vision port, using binoculars to look at the remaining satellite, now half buried in dust. It made a starting point, away from the unwelcome news he had and he tried to take a light tone, 'If you wanted a close scan, you should have left it where it was in the Tech lab.'

Nerves at a stretch, Koenig could pick up vibrations. He turned round slowly, 'This sudden "cheerfulness" tells me you came in to say something else. We're not going into orbit?'

Bergman's face told him he had guessed right, even before he said, 'No,' and went on, 'We should have gone to the planet after all.'

Koenig crossed his desk and sat heavily in the command chair. Making it easier for Bergman, he said, 'Somehow I don't think I'd like the people.'

'They gave us air.'

'Which will shrink into an ice cap when we leave the warmth of Ariel's sun. Alpha could be crushed.' He stopped. There was no need to spell it out to the scientific adviser. 'What about the corrosion proofing on the Eagle?'

'They've worked round the clock. It's ready.'

Koenig was out of his chair and away through Main Mission. Before Bergman reached a direct vision port, the Eagle's motors were rising to a howl.

Midday brought a tropical sun to Morrow's ragged shack, heat, if anything, was marginally higher than in the wrecked cabin under its insulating dust. Paul Morrow squatted beside Sandra and fanned her with a piece of thin panelling and talked all the time, 'First we organise a farm spread, mushroom farms, manna farms. Later there'll be roads and slowly, very slowly at first, the community will have a centre, an urban heart of great buildings. This will be the capital city of the new civilisation.'

Helena Russell heard it as she came in carrying specimens of the manna she had tested.

'I still can't be sure about it, Paul. On the other hand I can't find any positive reaction to make it unsafe. But you're right. It's the only chance we have. On balance, I think maybe we should risk it.'

'I never had any doubt.'

'When we get back, I can give it a thorough going

over, but . . .' Morrow cut in, 'We're not going back. This is our home. This is where we stay. Here we begin our new life.'

There was a nervous intensity about his voice that surprised Helena. She stood still watching him and his tone became more shrill as he went on, 'None of this has happened by chance. Think of it! We are given an atmosphere. There is a freak electric storm and we lose contact. There is a freak dust storm and we are buried. We are close to starvation and manna is sent from the heavens. The people on that planet have a purpose and I believe we too have one now.'

Sandra felt his strangeness and struggled to sit up and touch him. Carter, on the way in with a bundle of the manna, stopped in the doorway taking in the implications. Morrow went on, close to hysteria, 'This land will flow with milk and honey. We will build and settle and bring up children. We will multiply. Like the ancient peoples of Peru, who spread the human family across the Pacific in their fragile rafts, we also will launch out into space and spread humanity from one solar system to another.'

Alan Carter had heard enough. There was no need to look at the dawning knowledge on Helena's face. He made a practical expression of opinion, turning in the doorway and taking a drop kick at his bundle to boot it out into the dust.

Morrow was on to him like a fanatic, grabbing him from behind, twisting him round to face him with a madman's strength. 'That was sacred bread, Alan. That was sent to us in our time of need. You don't kick a gift horse in the teeth.' The voice notched to a scream, 'Down on your knees. Crawl to it. Pick it up.'

Struggling to break the grip, Carter said, 'Go pick your teeth.' He got an arm free and tried to fend off from Morrow's chest. But Morrow took it as a blow, sent in a savage jab that had Carter reeling back against the doorpost. Carter came on again, roused now and aiming to make a fight of it. But he was no match for Morrow's fortified strength.

Sandra called, 'Paul!'—but he was outside the reach of any appeal. He slammed Carter to the deck and jumped in for the kill.

Helena Russell saw how it would be and put herself in the way, 'Paul! Stop!'

He swept her aside, knelt down over Carter, lifted his head for a hammer blow.

Scrabbling to her feet, Helena grabbed for a hypo pack beside Sandra's bed. She had the gun out and was behind Morrow when his now hyper-sensitive nerves alerted him to the danger. Dropping Carter back to the deck, he was round in a flash, seizing her wrist before she could fire, forcing her fingers to open and drop the gun.

Voice full of menace, he said, 'Did you want to put me out?'

'No. It was for Alan. He's hurt.'

Inexorably, Morrow backed her to the wall, hands crawling up her chest and closing round the smooth column of her throat, eyes insane and murderous.

'You lie. It was for me. You would come between me and my destiny. No one stops me. No one.'

Outside, there was a high pitched scream and another, then a succession, until the noise was unbearable. Morrow paused, took away his hands, looked at them and ran outside. Helena followed massaging her throat. The moonscape had gotten a return visit. Ariel's gleaming satellites were dotted about like a minefield. They had gone into reverse. Faint streamers leading to the frill of fine tubes, showed what they were at. They had come to take the atmosphere back.

Morrow was beyond understanding. He ran to the nearest, touched it with reverence, called out, 'Here is your sign, Doctor. Look about you. The people of the planet Ariel are come again. It is the second coming.'

But he had lost his audience. Helena Russell had a sign of her own. Flying low in the distance, she could see something bulkier than a satellite. It was a searching Eagle coming across the horizon. For a moment she thought of alerting Morrow, then realised he might prevent her making any signal. Without a word, she turned away and ran for the crashed Eagle.

Koenig was flying at zero height. He had guessed that Eagle Two Eight must be well hidden in some dust bowl. Mathias in the pilot seat said, 'Atmospheric pressure's falling rapidly now, Commander. We're running out of time.'

Bergman called from Mission Control with the same story, 'We're losing atmosphere, John. The satellites are back in force.'

It was certainly true of the terrain they were crossing. Koenig said shortly, 'I can see them.'

On the surface, the effect of thinning air was hitting Helena Russell as she thrashed about in the passenger module for gas cylinders which had been restacked after the crash. Mouth open, she was drawing long quivering breaths as she hauled them out and used her last strength to open the valves.

Liquid gas hissing out and vapourising added to her problems and she had to stop, grabbing up a laser from the rack over the hatch as she stumbled out and moved her leaden limbs in a heroic jog trot. Ten paces off, she turned, aimed for the open hatch and sent a thin searing beam into the interior.

The Eagle made its last contribution to Moonbase Alpha, opening like a flower in time lapse with a dull muffled roar and sending a column of flame and debris into the failing sky. The blast hurled Helena

Russell on her back in the dust and she saw nothing of the spectacular.

Mathias scanning round one eighty degrees of arc picked up the marker and thumped Koenig's arm, 'Commander! Fifteen degrees right.'

Koenig veered in a virtuoso turn that had them strained in their harness and got it dead ahead.

He said, 'Good, Bob,' and threw in every erg of reserve power so that the Eagle sprang forward as though booted up the stern.

Helena was crawling, trying to stand and falling again, face bleeding from a blast wound, tunic in flapping shreds, lungs labouring to get a working ration of air.

In the hut, Carter was shaking his head from side to side like a dog and on his knees beside Sandra's bed. She was gasping for breath, 'Alan, what's happening to us?'

He hauled himself to the door. There was a column of smoke still rising from the wreck. Morrow was waving his arms, talking wildly to the satellites, his words lost in their continuing screams. Helena Russell had fallen again and Carter saw the movement. He stumbled out, reached her and tried to lift her. But he was too weak and fell across her legs.

The Eagle touched down in a whirlwind of dust and Mathias said urgently, 'Spacesuits, Commander. The atmosphere's thinning fast.'

Koenig was already in the hatch. 'No time.'

Carter, finding strength he should not have had, was on his feet and had Helena across his arms. Koenig tried to take her, but Carter was programmed to move and would not stop. He jerked out, 'Sandra. In the hut. She needs help.'

Mathias took Helena's shoulders. Koenig knew they would reach the Eagle and raced on. He was inside the hut and bending to pick up Sandra when hands grabbed him from behind and swung him round.

'Paul!'

'Leave her alone.'

'Paul. We don't have much time.' He turned again to lift her and Morrow's voice rose to a scream, 'I said leave her alone!'

Once more he grabbed Koenig and hurled him aside. Off balance, Koenig fell heavily gasping for breath and Morrow, panting now and holding his throat, shouted, 'We have laid the foundation stone of Mankind's future . . . The struggle will be long and hard . . .'

Koenig was on his feet, knowing there was no time at all, aiming to make a quick finish but Morrow had a maniac's strength and cunning. He dodged, struck hard and Koenig was flung back.

Rhetoric beat him. Instead of going in for the kill, he delivered another communique from his wandering, mind, 'Faint hearts . . . will not survive. But the blade of human endeavour . . . is tempered in the fire of the Universe.'

Koenig had time to pick his spot and was in with a punch that sent Morrow reeling against Sandra's bed. Her sudden scream penetrated the mists in his mind and he turned to look at her. Koenig was on him again, with a blow to the chin that split his knuckles and dropped Morrow like a log.

Bergman, working hard to find some profit in a situation that had gone sour, was glad to take his box into Main Mission. Grinning like a pleased gnome, he held it up for all to see. Morrow's mushrooms were doing well. He said, 'It's food. Good food. Fantastically rich in second class protein and many essential vitamins. There's no limit to the crop we can get, once we've ironed out all the hallucinogenic traces.'

Helena said, 'Sorry I didn't isolate them sooner, Paul.'

Morrow, still looking haggard, managed his normal cheerful smile. He put an arm carefully round Sandra's bulky strapping, 'Not to worry. It wasn't a bad trip. Except for the ending.'

Koenig said sententiously, 'In situations like that you discover who your friends are.'

A bleep from a monitor broke across their talk. Tanya called, 'The satellite, Commander. It's moving!'

She threw a picture on the main scanner. It was true. The first and last visitor from Ariel was stirring in its dust bed.

Carter said, 'It's leaving us.'

Koenig for one, was glad to see it go. He began, 'The sooner the—' but he was interrupted.

A sing song, electronic voice was making the first direct communication they had been given, 'We are neither benevolent nor malevolent, Commander Koenig . . .'

The satellite was hovering above Alpha and a beam of light was streaming down to Main Mission, pulsing as the voice went on, 'Our absolute need was to prevent you from penetrating the atmosphere of our planet. We were fearful that fate would put you in orbit round our sun. So we created conditions you wanted, so that you would not further disturb us.'

It was a lot to digest. Koenig broke the silence, 'Can you hear me?'

'And understand your thoughts.'

'Then you must know we came in peace?'

'We believe your intentions were good but we have been watching the progress of your world since its beginning. Your human nature is such that we could not afford to take the risk.'

It had made its definitive answer. The light dimmed out and the satellite moved again with ever increasing acceleration to dwindle away towards the distant planet.

Koenig said, 'Kill the lights, Paul.'

Main Mission was plunged in darkness. A faint red glow came from the direct vision ports and all hands looked out over the barren moonscape, as their temporary sun slipped away over the horizon.

John Koenig, standing with Helena said, 'At least let's enjoy the last sunset.'

CHAPTER FIVE

Somebody once said that work was a great therapy and John Koenig could agree with it. Looking round Main Mission with all systems go and a professional job to be done, he reckoned that his crew were coming out of the numbing disappointment they had felt and were happier than at any time over the last months.

The Main Scanner was sewn with brilliants as it tracked over the star map. Moving across the endless panorama, two Eagles staked out the human claim.

Alan Carter's voice crossed the wasteland and Sandra brought up an inset picture of the command module of Eagle One. He was reading it from his instrument spread, 'Object's course and trajectory holding steady. Sensor readings growing stronger.'

Kano affirmed from his computer console, 'Positive analysis, Commander. Object approaching us is artificially powered.'

Bergman looked hard at Koenig. 'A ship?'

There was no reply. Koenig was not ready to commit himself. It would not be long before they had more data and Sandra Benes, as though chiming in on his thinking, said, 'Nine seconds to visual.'

Koenig said, 'Eagles One and Two maintain your approach.'

Carter's laconic 'Check, Commander,' was followed by a quick interjection from Steve Abrams in the pilot slot of Eagle Two, 'The scanners have it now, Commander.'

Koenig leaned both hands on the back of Sandra's chair and stared at the big screen, waiting for the pictures to show and Sandra counted down, 'Two seconds . . .'

Out of the billions of light specks, there was one separating out, a tiny hurrying fragment moving towards them from the vast reaches of space. Electronic gear locked on, enlarged it to a recognisable size and shape and landed it for them like a silver fish. There was no longer any doubt. They had a visitor. It was a hurrying spacer.

John Koenig's reaction was immediate and positive, 'Eagles One and Two, activate onboard defensive systems.'

Carter's reaction time showed his complete concentration. He was an extension of his machine, while the harmonics were still vibrating, he was flipping switches in a row and calling again. 'We're picking up a signal, Commander.'

'Relay it.'

A low pulsing droned out from the repeaters in Main Mission and Koenig said sharply, 'Kano?'

The computer operator swivelled to face him, 'It's some kind of call sign, Commander.'

'Acknowledge.'

Kano went to work and the atmosphere in Main Mission was electric. The signal cut out, leaving a sudden silence. Helena Russell, running a continuous medical monitoring scan on the Eagles' personnel, involuntarily put a hand to her mouth as though she was expecting an announcement of mind shattering importance.

When it came, it was like calling a lover and getting an answering service. A distorted metallic voice punched out a prepared statement, 'THIS IS THE VOICE OF VOYAGER ONE.'

Sandra had a close shot of the ship to back it. There was no doubt the voice had gotten it right. On the nose cone, stylised outlines of a human male and his female consort symbolised the point of origin in Earth planet.

The voice went on, 'OUR SHIP IS UNMANNED AND UNARMED. WE COME ON A MISSION OF PEACE AND GOODWILL.'

The text was friendly enough but Bergman's reaction was near to panic. Grabbing Koenig's arm, he could only say, 'A *Voyager* ship!'

Koenig was ahead of him, calling urgently, 'Carter!' Abrams! Pull away!'

Maybe he was already too late. Seen on the scanner, both Eagles were in trouble. Yawing and vibrating, they were running out of control.

Helena Russell called, 'Both pilots under severe stress.'

Koenig tried again, 'Do you read me, Eagles One and Two?'

A heavy rumbling was building from the repeaters. Carter, sweating with effort was fighting to pull his Eagle in a turn. He jerked out, 'We're under attack ... Alpha ...'

Abrams cut in, 'Eagle Two out of control.'

They could see it. The vibration was shaking Eagle Two into scrap. Abrams rocking violently in his command chair was getting no joy from any control. They heard him again, forcing the words from clenced teeth, 'Eagle . . . Two . . . not . . . responding.'

Eagle Two was spiralling, breaking up, still moving towards Voyager, superstructure pulsing like a beating heart. But Carter was making out, he was turning and the noise from the vibrating hull was less.

Abrams's voice was notched up to a scream, as though to compete with the pandemonium in his command cabin. 'Can't turn . . . The ship . . . Falling apart.'

They saw Eagle Two buck violently, slamming Abrams back and forward against his straps. No structure made by man could take the punishment. A fracture line opened up, spread like a torn paper and Eagle Two became molecular trash among the interstellar dust.

Helena Russell's monitor screens confirmed it for the human cargo. Negative. Negative. Where human life had been, there was the long silence. There was silence to match it in Main Mission as the personnel came to terms with sudden death. Voyager One's computer voice, becoming clearer, said evenly, 'THIS IS THE VOICE OF VOYAGER ONE. GREETINGS FROM THE PEOPLE OF PLANET EARTH.'

Paul Morrow said tersely, 'We've lost ship to base communication.'

Looking at the inside of Carter's labouring Eagle, Koenig doubted whether it would matter. Alan Carter had a thin line of blood trickling down his nose and seemed to make no effort to stop himself being shaken about by the random moves of his craft. Except to say that it was still holding together, there was nothing good in the picture.

Helena's monitors had gone dead. She said, 'No life signs. I hope it's the onboard instruments.'

Watching closely, Koenig saw a flicker from Carter's face, a grimace of pain. He said urgently, 'Paul. Keep communications open.'

Carter was hauling himself erect in his chair. They saw him move, painfully, slowly, to get a grip on the manual controls. It was a lonely struggle with nothing anybody could do to ease the burden.

Morrow said incredulously, 'My God. He'll do it. Eagle One's flight pattern's stabilising.' His surprise was shared by Carter himself, who was looking round his cabin as though he was seeing it fresh after resurrection. The rumbling noise faded. Eagle One was in level flight.

Sandra, smiling after the tension said triumphantly 'Eagle One, Commander,' and Koenig hit a switch.

'Alan?'

The voice was weak, but all systems go, 'How am I doing?'

'Automatic's shot to hell. Can you work on manual?'

'I think so, Commander. Did Abrams make it?'

'No.'

'What hit us?'

'The Queller Drive.'

It would make sense to Carter, but others were not so far ahead. Koenig answered the unspoken questions, 'Voyager One is powered by two types of engine; normal rocket motors and the Queller Drive—an automatic engine that delivers incredible speed from a stream of fast neutrons.'

Paul Morrow remembered the programme and was suddenly angry, 'Yes. Fast neutrons spewed out into space, annihilating everything in their path. You could as well stand in the middle of an atomic strike. If it comes too close, we'll be burned up. If it passes at a distance we'll be polluted by neutron fall out. It's death either way. We've got to blast it out of the sky, Commander.'

Koenig was listening and believing. The same analysis had run through his head and it looked like plain logic. They both turned to Victor Bergman, who had been at the computer console and was reading a print-out as he hurried over to them, 'John. Listen to this. It's all here. Voyager One. Launched 1985. Mission: to probe the Galaxy for signs of intelligent life; to document habitable solar systems; to advertise man's presence in the Galaxy.'

He looked at them both, clearly impressed by the scientific angles, 'And now, would you believe it, we see it on its return trip? Fifteen years later! It's an epic. What an achievement.'

His enthusiasm was not catching. Helena Russell said flatly, 'It's a threat to all life on this base.'

He conceded that, 'There is danger from the Queller Drive.'

Morrow was indignant, 'Danger? If we all climbed into lead caskets under twelve feet of concrete, we'd still burn like fried onions!'

'Think of the scientific information in that ship.'

Helena said, 'My concern is about our lives.'

There was no doubt left for Morrow. 'We *must* destroy it.'

Bergman looked from one face to another. He was in a minority of one, but still batting. 'No. It's unthinkable.'

Koenig played for time and called in Kano, 'How long do we have?'

'Limit of safety, eleven hours, Commander.'

'Eleven hours. All right. That gives us a breathing space.'

Helena Russell, thinking he was agreeing with Bergman said urgently, 'For what? We have no protection. We must stop it.'

Carter's voice broke in. Working now with his old flair, he was holding Eagle One on a course, 'Eagle One on approach. We should make it. But keep your heads down.'

It eased the tension. Koenig answered, 'We'll be waiting. Good luck, Alan.' He turned to Morrow, 'Crash crews on standby.'

As he went up the steps to his command office, Morrow was already setting it up. 'Emergency crew to launch pad four. Stand by crash unit one.'

Moonbase Alpha clicked smoothly into gear. A crash tender Eagle rose to the pad and a boarding tube snaked out to give access. Koenig watched the sequence as he listened to Bergman still pushing his theory and Helena Russell making a bid for practical common sense.

'So what are you suggesting, Victor?'

'Simply this. We must try to get hold of the information that Voyager contains. We can't just blow it up out of hand.'

'What do you say to that Helena?'

'We can't take any chance at all with the Queller Drive. We know what it does.'

Bergman was impatient, 'Listen. For fifteen years Voyager has been photographing other planets, analysing their atmosphere, detailing all forms of life, recording temperatures, gravities. It would take us a hundred years to learn what Voyager already knows.'

Helena conceded that much, 'I can accept that. The information on Voyager is probably our best chance of survival. But you can't get round the Queller Drive.'

Koenig said slowly, 'Victor. Voyager has *two* engines, right?'

'Correct.'

'Chemical, conventional rockets for launching and landing. The Queller Drive takes over to cover the vast distances of interstellar space. It made star travel possible. But Voyager One is unmanned. How does it switch from rocket engines to the Queller Drive and back again?'

'Computer control.'

'So?'

'I think I see what you're getting at . . .'

'Look. Can we alter the programme on Voyager's computer? Can we modify its instructions so that it shuts down the Queller Drive?'

Helena Russell was positive and looked as though she would like to thump sense into Koenig's head.

'We cannot risk it.'

But Bergman looked pleased, 'Can we afford not to risk it?'

Once again Carter provided a safety valve. He was down on the pad and Morrow reported it. 'Eagle One is in.'

Koenig had been looking at Helena, conscious that this time they were on opposite sides of a fence and not liking it. He said, 'Carter?'

'In one piece.'

'Good.'

Helena intervened, 'Have him report to the medi-centre.' On her way out, she gave Koenig a straight look and put it on the line, 'You want to save Voyager—even at the risk of all our lives.'

'We have to try.'

'In that case, we'd better find out all we can about fast neutrons.'

'We're not in any danger . . . yet.'

'No. Not yet.'

Turning abruptly, her blonde hair swinging, she went out. If she could have slammed the hatch, she would have.

In the medicentre, she switched in a repeater to get any information that was coming into Main Mission. She heard Bergman make a request for computer service and heard its plummy tones. 'Your request on fast neutron effects. Detailed information not banked. Records suggest we have a resident specialist. Contact Doctor Ernst Linden, Experimental Physics Laboratory.'

She thought that would please Bergman at least. Linden was one of his own team. Not that anybody saw much of him and she had difficulty putting a face to the name. He was a quiet, self-effacing type, who hardly ever left the confines of his lab. Out of curiosity, she turned up his medical record and looked at his identity block. The photograph showed him to be an elderly, distinguished looking man. It was strange that she had not made any contact. That would have to be remedied.

The maestro himself was absorbed in a problem. He had turned his own corner of Alpha into an exotic retreat for experimental science. Remnants of a long succession of experiments on propulsion and automatic handling devices hung about like surrealist decorations. Currently, he was making delicate adjustments to a piece of apparatus, watched by Jim Haines his young assistant.

Justifying himself, Haines said, 'See what I mean? It should work but it doesn't.'

Linden gave him a good humoured look, 'Of course, it couldn't be the energy cell duct?'

'Not a chance . . . Well . . .' Haines slapped his forehead with the heel of his hand, 'All right. You know damn well it is.'

'Just a suggestion.'

'I know your suggestions. I'll go get one.'

On the way out, he passed Helena Russell coming in. She was making up for lost time. Linden went on working and she had to speak to get attention, which given her spectacular figure was unusual.

'Doctor Linden.'

He looked up, nodded and went back to work, putting in a deft adjustment, before he straightened up and proved that he knew who it was even if he would have traded her any day for a transistor. 'Doctor Russell.'

'I need your help. Computer referred me to you. It seems you're the local expert on fast neutrons.'

'I have some small knowledge of the subject. What is the problem?'

'An emergency situation. A fast neutron source is approaching us from space.' There was no doubt that she was getting more attention, but there was no verbal response. She went on, 'An early probe ship, sent from Earth. A Voyager class vessel. Voyager One to be exact.'

Linden was gripping the edge of his work top to stay on his feet. Voice in a harsh whisper, he repeated the information for his data acquisition networks which were clearly finding it difficult to take, 'Voyager One?'

If he had been in Main Mission, he would have had ocular proof. Voyager One was featured on the main scanner ploughing its solitary furrow over the star map. Victor Bergman, watching it, said to Kano, 'The problem is to get access to the Voyager command circuits. Then we can give the computer new instructions. I want a link up through our computer programmer to Voyager One. See what you can do, Kano.'

'Check, Professor.'

When his visitor had gone, Linden sat heavily at his desk and made no move when Haines came back. Haines began to unpack components, slamming them one by one on his bench. Finally he had to break the silence. 'You've heard the big news? There's a Voyager ship out there.'

Linden was away in private speculation and Haines said again, 'Did you hear me, Doctor?'

'Yes . . .'

'They're playing games with the Queller Drive. It'll be like Voyager Two all over again. They've forgotten everything and remembered nothing. Know what they aim to do? They want to stop it . . . shut down its drive!'

This time he had a reaction. Linden hauled himself to his feet and spoke more to himself than to his assistant. 'They can't do that!'

Before Haines could speak again, he was out through the hatch walking with quick nervous strides. He moved to Main Mission where the action was and stood unobtrusively at the back of the crowd listening to Bergman who was trying to talk to Voyager One's computer.

'Voyager One. This is the voice of Earth Space Authority. Do you acknowledge?'

'ACKNOWLEDGED.'

'Stand by to allow access to your command file.'

'REQUEST REFUSED.'

Bergman tried again. 'This is the voice of Earth Space Control.'

'ACKNOWLEDGED.'

'Voyager One. Delete Command file and stand by for fresh instructions.'

'REQUEST REFUSED.'

'On what grounds?'

'UNAUTHORISED INSTRUCTIONS.'

'You are *ordered* to delete your command instructions.'

'REQUEST REFUSED. PRIME DIRECTIVES CANNOT BE ALTERED UNLESS PRECEDED BY DELETE CODE.'

The signal note from Voyager One changed key and Kano tracked on his console to keep steady on the frequency. Voyager One came in loud and clear, 'THIS IS THE VOICE OF VOYAGER ONE.

GREETINGS FROM THE PEOPLE OF EARTH PLANET.'

Kano said disgustedly, 'It's just not interested, Professor.'

Voyager One was starting off again on its Galactic greeting and Koenig said, 'Cut it.'

Thinking aloud, Bergman said, 'There's got to be a way to crack its delete code.'

Unexpectedly, he got an answer. Stepping forward quietly, Linden said, 'There is, Professor.'

He was composed, very dignified and went on with an authority that drew every eye. 'The command controls will only respond to precise signals. Persistent attempts to stop it in any other way could trigger its destruct mechanism.'

Koenig asked, 'What do you know about it?'

'I was . . . involved . . . in the Voyager Project.'

Bergman was suspicious, 'I do not recall a Doctor Linden . . .'

'If you check my personal index you will find that long before I came to Alpha my name was Queller.'

Whatever his impact had been before, there was no doubt he had made his mark now. First to recover, Koenig said, 'Are you telling us that you are Ernst Queller?'

'That is correct. I designed the Queller Drive.'

The top brass of Moonbase Alpha had a blow up of Voyager One as a backdrop to their conference as they sat round the table in Koenig's command office.

Helena, still trying to come to terms with it said 'Ernst Queller?'

Kano, liking accuracy said, 'As was. The name was changed to Linden before ever he was assigned to Alpha.'

'But no one knew.'

Koenig said, 'He was cleared for duty on Alpha. If he chose not to reveal who he was, that was his right. Everyone has the right to that much privacy.'

Paul Morrow went for first principles, 'He may have changed his name, but nothing can change what he did.'

There was even a more recent charge on the sheet and Carter put a finger on it, 'His Queller Drive killed Abrams.'

Morrow added it up, 'That's one more to his score, but I'm thinking of the second ship in the programme, Voyager Two. The Queller Drive cut in too soon . . .'

Interrupting, Victor Bergman made a plea for science, 'It *was* an error, Paul. Something went wrong . . .'

'Two hundred people died, that's what went wrong. A whole community wiped out. My father was one of them. I know something went wrong.'

Anger was mounting with memory and Koenig brought his conference back to the realities, 'All right, Paul. This is specially hard for you. But we are not here now to pass moral judgement on Ernst Queller. We're here to decide if Ernst Linden can help us.'

It gained him no credit with Helena Russell. Not meeting his eyes, she said bitterly, 'You would put the survival of Alpha in the hands of that man?'

Koenig ignored her, 'Victor, can you guarantee to shut down the Queller Drive in time?'

'Guarantee? No.'

'All right. Let's have Linden in.'

Koenig swivelled in his chair and used his commlock to open the hatch. Linden was waiting calm and composed in spite of the circle of accusing faces. He walked steadily to the head of the table and faced Koenig.

John Koenig said, 'Doctor Linden, we need the information Voyager can give us. I want to know if you can shut down the Queller Drive so that we can reach that information. Please think carefully. I want to know if you can do it with the facilities we have available on Moonbase. I want to know if you can do it in the time we have left.' He looked at Kano for the latest figure.

Kano said, 'Nine hours, ten minutes.' Koenig went on, 'Yes or no?'

There was no hesitation from Linden. He said simply, 'I believe I can.'

'Yes or no?'

'Commander Koenig, twenty years ago, I would have given you my guarantee. Now, all I can say is I will do everything I can.'

The ball was back definitely in Koenig's court and he looked steadily at Linden's calm face trying to discard everything he knew for a new estimate of the man. At last, he said, 'Thank you.'

It was a vote of confidence and Linden took it as that. When he had gone, Koenig looked round the ring of faces, 'I'm going along with him. Paul, keep this close. I don't want his real identity widely known.'

Morrow snapped his notebook shut. 'Not even Haines? Jim Haines lost both parents on account of Queller. He should know who he's working with.'

Koenig was dubious about that one. If he could have seen into the experimental lab he might have been more convinced that he was right. Jim Haines was currently having enough problems with the device he was building. Linden's rapid instructions had left him behind, but he was soldiering on with blind faith in his chief.

Linden was covering sheet after sheet with equations and did not look up when Haines said, 'Are you sure you know what you're doing? I don't.'

'Just build it, Jim.'

In Main Mission, Carter was working on a contingency plan and Koenig, after watching Voyager One moving inexorably towards Alpha, asked him to brief him on it.

The chief pilot had a coloured chart on the scanner and had it worked out. 'It's a three phase operation, Commander. I've hatched in three zones. As soon as Voyager enters the green area, our Eagles go to automatic alert. If it makes the yellow band, we move into position here. The moment it nudges over into the red we blast it with everything we've got.'

Koenig nodded. It looked good. He said, 'Begin countdown.'

Digits began to slide behind the windows of the countdown clock, with a solid clunk on every full minute. It showed seven hours on the nose, a symbolic number. As Koenig watched, it flipped down to 6-59 with a sweep second hand making indecent haste to whip them along to annihilation. When he visited Linden and Haines in their workshop it was down to 4-17 and still busy as a flea.

They had knocked up an impressive three-dimensional artefact that sent flickers through an array of neon tubes and was emitting an audio pulse. It looked impressive enough. Koenig said quietly to Haines, 'I'd like to speak to Doctor Linden.'

Linden answered for himself, straightening from the bench and nodding to Haines, 'Jim, those quartz components. They should be ready by now.'

Haines went away to check and Linden was ready, anticipating Koenig's question.

'It will be finished on time. As soon as the circuit pattern is complete I can override the command instructions and shut down the drive.'

'Possibilities of failure?'

Linden was confident, almost boastful, 'None. I created the Queller Drive. All I need is time.'

'Do you need more men?'

'No. Haines and I can do it alone, faster.'

There was a defensive element in the reply that made Koenig ask, 'I hope you're not trying to prove something, Doctor?'

'You and I both want to stop Voyager. I suggest you leave me to do it, Commander.'

Koenig debated. There was not much area of choice. It was his decision and with Helena still against him and gone icily cool he was feeling somewhat isolated. He spun on his heel and returned to Main Mission.

Carter was deploying his Eagles. One by one they were rising to their launch pads and receiving their crew complement. On the Main Scanner, Voyager One was clear to the last detail like a still picture.

Carter said, 'Eagles Six, Nine and Ten. Launch positions.'

Pilots were answering in sequence.

'Eagle Six. Ready for launch.'

'Eagle Ten. In position.'

'Eagle Nine. Ready for launch.'

Carter was watching the countdown clock. From two hours one minute, it changed with a definitive clunk to two hours dead and a green tell tale glowed into life. On the instant he was calling his pilots, 'Eagles Six, Nine and Ten. Condition green now operative. Go!'

Vibrations ran through Moonbase Alpha as the motors delivered and the Eagles clawed themselves over the moonscape. He saw them wheel and form a flight pattern and spoke again, 'We're watching you. Good luck all.'

Silence fell on Main Mission. There was nothing anybody wanted to say. There was the clock to watch and the leaden minutes sheared themselves off like so much waste metal. In the experimental lab, Linden's concentration was absolute. Beads of sweat were standing out on his forehead. Once he looked at the repeater and saw the clock at one-forty six. Then it knocked down the single hour, the green light blinked out and came on again in yellow.

Sandra Benes said unnecessarily, 'One hour to interception.'

John Koenig nodded to Carter and he called his Eagles. 'Control to Eagles Six, Nine and Ten. Condition Yellow. Move to intercept positions.'

They saw them fan out in a wide arc with Voyager One arrowing in on its undeviating course.

Koenig said, 'Anything from Linden?'

Bergman looking anxious shook his head.

In fact Linden was running a preliminary test on his brainchild, tapping out a sequence from his console and watching the heap glow and blip to his tune.

Haines looked at it in simple disbelief. 'Will it work?'

'It will work.'

Linden had almost worked himself to a standstill. As he went to the bench for some final adjustments he was talking to himself. 'Nothing can stop us now. We can override the onboard computer, the security codes are irrelevant. We can shut down the Drive any time we like.'

Haines watched him with his mind suddenly switched on a new thought. He said, 'What? Override the onboard computer? Security codes irrelevant? How did we do that?'

'You don't understand, Jim. We have recreated the control pattern for the Queller Drive.'

'That's not possible.' The idea in Haines's head was crystalising out into a terrible certainty. 'There's only one man who could do that. Only one man had the knowledge.' He was close to Linden, grabbing him by the lapels of his coat as the truth became plain. 'Tell me who you are.'

'Please Jim.'

'Hell! Tell me! I want to hear it from you. Tell me.'

Linden's face was grey. There was no need for speech. Haines was shaking him in a blaze of anger. 'You're Ernst Queller. That's right, isn't it?'

All the tension of the last hours and the sense of betrayal that he should have given loyalty and even affection to this man burned in a red tide through Haines's mind. He threw Linden away from him across the room.

Linden stumbled backwards, fought for balance, hit the bench with the back of his legs and flailed wildly with his arms. There was a blinding flash and the crack of exploding tubes. Linden pitched forward face down. Haines suddenly ice cold looked at the wreckage.

The countdown clock clunked the demise of another minute. It stood accusingly at 0-45.

CHAPTER SIX

Ernst Linden was out cold, face like set wax. Watching Helena and Bob Mathias go to work with a mobile trolley of medical gear, Koenig reckoned bitterly that they were wasting the precious minutes still pounding out of the clock.

'How is he?'

Helena Russell connected another electrode and answered obliquely, profile averted, 'Fractured ribs. Shock. All set, Bob. Switch on.'

As the energy flowed, Linden stirred. She said, 'Again,' and Linden's eyes opened slowly.

Koenig said, 'How did this happen?'

This time he got a full face response, but it was more of a slow burn. She was too angry to speak and merely looked away towards Haines.

Haines himself was still overcome by the enormity of what he had done. He said haltingly, 'Commander, believe me . . . I didn't intend. . . .'

Koenig's voice was like a whip crack, 'Stupid. You've destroyed the only chance we had . . .'

Unexpectedly, Haines had an ally. Linden called weakly, 'Commander . . . Please. It was not his fault.'

Haines started an apology, 'I'm sorry . . .' but he was cut short by Koenig, 'Get out!'

Linden was trying again, sweating with pain as he tried to move himself off the deck, 'Voyager . . .'

'Don't concern yourself with Voyager. We can't save it now.'

There was silence. Koenig went to the work bench to inspect the damage. To his eye, they had a write-off. Linden shifted himself with a superhuman effort to get a look at the clock. They had thirty-four minutes. He said, 'I can. There's still time.'

He was on his feet, holding his rib cage, face twisted by pain, dragging himself to join Koenig at the bench. 'Don't destroy it yet!'

'Right now there are three Eagles lining up their sights on Voyager.'

'I must finish what I started.'

Helena could hardly believe what she was hearing. She said, coldly, 'Why? You're not doing it for us. You're doing it to resolve some kind of personal conflict. You're fighting a battle no-one gives a damn about.'

Linden ignored her, 'May I resume my work now?'

The communications post blipped urgently for attention and Sandra Benes appeared on screen, 'Commander. Main Mission. Urgent.'

Koenig was at the hatch before the picture faded. As a parting shot, he said to Mathias, 'Do what you can to prevent this man killing himself.'

All eyes in Main Mission were on the operations scanner. Three bright specks had materialised way behind Voyager. Sandra said, 'Three objects, Commander. Following Voyager's course.'

Kano's computer started to jibber and Kano had a print-out to read, 'Positive identification, Commander. They're spacers. Flight path identical with Voyager One. Heading for Alpha.'

Sandra did some delicate timing and they had it plain on the main scanner. Voyager One was zooming in with three hurrying specks closing on her trail.

In the experimental lab, Linden, face a mask of sweat was driving himself to repair his damaged transmitter. Reluctantly, Helena Russell gave him some credit in human terms, whatever the motive, he was a fighter. As he stopped, racked with a surge of pain, she came forward with a charged hypo gun and gave him another pain killing shot.

As his breath steadied, he said, 'Thank you.'

'You can't take much more of this.'

'I know what I'm doing.'

'Do you?' Her voice was less challenging. She was almost apologetic, 'Don't you see? It'll have to be destroyed. You're killing yourself for nothing.'

'You wouldn't understand.'

The countdown clock clicked hitting fourteen. He switched on. There was still a small segment of the circuit giving no joy. He went on working at it.

When the clock hit five, Koenig was ready to give Carter the clear. Paul Morrow watching the big screen said, 'Those ships are definitely following Voyager.'

Whatever the reason was, Koenig knew it was secondary to their present problem. He dismissed it from his thinking and listened to the exchange between Eagle Six and Carter.

'Eagles maintaining intercept positions.'

'Check. Hold it there.'

Linden, blind to anything but his circuits was ready for another dry run. Even Helena felt his triumph as the whole device glowed into life. He went to his console, tapped a trial sequence, put his head on his hands and drew deep quivering breaths.

Carter called evenly, 'Three minutes to intercept.'

Main Mission was tense. Voyager One filled the big screen.

Carter called, 'Eagles to firing positions.'

Responses came in from his pilots, 'Eagle Six Copy.'

'Eagle Nine Copy.'

'Eagle Ten Copy.'

'Lock weapons.'

They answered again and Carter, ready for the moment of truth looked across at Koenig. The countdown clock hit 1 and the last seconds began to flick past. The yellow tell-tale died and the window glowed red.

Carter was ready to fire and Koenig intervened sharply, 'Wait Alan.'

'We can't . . .'

Kano confirmed it, 'Voyager One now in space area red.'

A slight rumbling noise began to build and every head in Main Mission turned to Koenig.

Morrow said, 'Commander!'

Eagle Six came in with the pilot's voice hard edged and anxious. 'Waiting for instructions to fire, Alpha!'

Alan Carter looked at Koenig's set face and voiced the appeal that was in every head, 'You must give the order to fire, Commander. Now!'

'I said wait.'

The rumbling increased. They were being held in the path of an unstoppable juggernaut. Only ingrained discipline and the long habit of accepting Koenig's decision was keeping them at their desks.

Sandra Benes spoke like a zombie, 'Countdown minus fifty seconds.'

The communications post blipped and Linden's haggard face joined the symposium. 'I'm ready. I need computer link up.'

Carter's voice cracked out, 'It's too late.'

But Koenig was already giving the go-ahead to Kano, 'All right, Kano. Link him up.'

In the experimental lab, Helena was watching the final stages of an incredible endurance effort. Linden's machine was pulsing and glowing like a monstrous heart. The pay-off was at hand and she could see that the man himself was almost overcome by all the memories and implications of what he had achieved. He was bowed over the console almost reluctant to make the final notes.

She came up behind him and said sincerely, 'Good luck.'

It was the trigger he needed to get him in action for the last phase. He looked at her, managed a wry smile and began to tap out rapid sequences on the console keyboard with a firm and positive hand. Responding to the master touch, the circuit pattern changed pitch and key and began to talk persuasively to the onboard computer on the hurrying Voyager One.

Main Mission was still under stress. Vibration was undiminished. The electronic voice of Voyager One's computer came in almost as an insult, 'THIS IS THE VOICE OF VOYAGER ONE.' But there was a change, something was throwing it out of kilter. It began to distort, accelerating as though it was determined to say its piece, 'GREETINGS. GREETINGS FROM THE PEOPLE OF EARTH.' It rose in a scream of gobbledegook and then cut out leaving a stunned silence.

Linden was still totally concentrated, hammering away at his complicated sequences, watching the impressive display on his flickering device as though mesmerised by it. Suddenly there was a change. He was over the hill and the response patterns levelled off to a low steady pulse.

Far away, Voyager One's frenetic acceleration had eased down. Chemical rocket motors had taken over the drive. He was exhausted, slumping forward over his console, hands slack.

In Main Mission the rumbling and the vibration

died away. Personnel looked at each other straining to hear what was no longer there.

Sandra called Koenig, 'Commander!'

Koenig was ahead of her, but waited to hear her confirm what he guessed.

'The Queller Drive. It's shut down!'

The communications post blipped and it was Linden. He had hauled himself together to make his report. Face looking ghastly on the screen he articulated slowly like a man in a coma, 'You took a chance, Commander. I am very grateful.'

Koenig said, 'So am I.'

'Where would you like Voyager One to land?'

'Launch pad four.'

The screen blanked. Koenig turned to Carter. 'Alan. Keep those Eagles in position.' Without waiting for a reply he began talking to his chief executive, making everything seem normal, giving them all an ongoing task to ease down the tension. 'Paul, prepare for boarding Voyager One as soon as she hits the deck.'

It had become a routine chore. Escorted by an Eagle outrider, Voyager One eased itself into a perfect approach line for its designated pad and came in with a burst of retro. The moment it touched down on its hydraulic jacks the engines cut. It looked innocent and beautiful under the floods, a triumph of engineering skill, a perfect thing in its own field. A boarding tube snaked out like an umbilical cord, giving access and symbolically asserting that its long lonely mission was over.

Linden was looking more human. The haunting anxiety had drained from his eyes. He could even see Helena Russell and make a human contact. He smiled at her and she said gently, 'You've done your job. Now I've got to do mine. Sick bay for you.'

He would have argued, but he could see that although she was no longer an enemy, she was determined about it. He shrugged and allowed her to help him to walk to the hatch.

Main Mission staff were trying hard to erase any impression they might have given that they were critical of Koenig.

Carter said deferentially, 'Voyager One ready for boarding, Commander.'

Koenig called off the patrolling Eagle, 'Stand down Eagle Five.'

They were a long way from being out of the wood. There could be tougher decisions to make yet.

Bergman said, 'The three alien ships are still closing.'

It had never been out of his mind and he looked at Carter's console, 'Keep watching, Alan.' Then he took Bergman on a sick visit.

Helena was looking more friendly when he asked, 'How is he making out?'

'He's taken a tremendous hammering.'

She led them along to Linden's bed. He was awake, looking relaxed and showed almost boyish embarrassment when Koenig said, 'Thank you.'

Another thought struck Koenig and he voiced it, 'The ship is now ready to enter. You should be the first to board her. What do you think, Helena? Is he fit to get up?'

Her eyes told him that she appreciated the gesture he was making. Her voice had its old warmth as she said, 'No. But I don't think I can stop him.'

'You can come along and keep an eye on him.'

Koenig kept his word. When the boarding tube clunked into place on Voyager's main hatch, he stepped aside ceremonially for Linden to do the honours.

Ernst Linden drew himself up, looked at each one in turn and walked forward, pressed a switch and the hatch sliced open as though it was a factory fresh model. They followed him on board into a spacious interior, eerily empty of human personnel.

Although unmanned, Voyager was a prototype for future passenger ships on interstellar passage. There were swivel chairs in the command cabin waiting for a crew, living quarters fitted out for those who were to come, future ghosts of the unborn. Koenig was impressed and looked at Linden with open admiration.

Too moved to speak, Linden crossed to the main control panel and stood looking at the superstructure. The others joined him. Scrawled on a flat panel were three names. CHARLES BORGES NEILL CAMERON ERNST QUELLER.

Speaking to Helena, Linden said shyly, 'My colleagues. We were all quite young.' He moved switches on the console below and went on simply, 'The Drive is now safe, Commander. This is very strange. Very strange for me to be in here again. As you see it was designed to carry crews at a later stage when men had developed the techniques of interstellar travel. But it was not to be. Well, where would you like to begin? The data is in those banks over there.'

A blip came from Koenig's commlock and he pulled it from his belt. On the miniature screen Paul Morrow appeared looking anxious. 'Commander, we're picking up a lot of magnetic activity inside Voyager One.'

It surprised Linden. He turned to the main console and checked instrumentation. He said, 'But that's not possible. The ship is completely deactivated.'

A pinging noise repeated on a two second beat and close to orchestral A, filled the cabin. Morrow called again. 'Intensity building rapidly now!'

The noise increased. Helena Russell, hands to her ears said 'John,' and went close to Koenig.

A thin column of light was standing like an instant prop from the deck to the roof of the command cabin.

It widened, blocked itself out in a brilliant cube. As they watched it became opaque and appeared solid as a marble block. Changing all the time, it cleared again and a face began to form deep in the mass.

It was humanoid, but strangely alien, fierce, bony with an enlarged cranium. Eyes glared angrily from deep sockets, looking at them in turn as though taking information for a black book. The thin feline mouth moved and the voice was speaking inside their heads, ringing, authoritative, each word carefully separated.

'Who speaks for you?'

Koenig took half a pace forward, 'I am John Koenig, Commander of this colony.'

'John Koenig you are communicating with Aarchon. I am Aarchon, Chief Justifier of the Federated Worlds of Sidon.' The way he told it, it was a good thing to be; but Koenig needed more information. He asked, 'What is your purpose here?'

Aarchon liked to ask the questions himself and ignored it. 'Are you citizens of the planet Earth?'

'That is so.'

The grim lines on the talking head deepened. 'Do you accept responsibility for the primitive craft known as Voyager One?'

'On behalf of the people of planet Earth, yes.'

'Then your colony, in keeping with your world must bear the judgement of Sidon.'

It was very clear which way the judgement was tending. Aarchon had not made the trip to hand out some Galactic prize. Aarchon went on, 'Your craft, Voyager One intruded into the Sidon worlds on the outer Galaxy . . .'

Unable to keep silent any longer, Linden stepped towards the cube, 'It came in peace. It was a peaceful mission.'

The head in the cube swivelled on its axis to fix the speaker with a hard glare. Aarchon's voice was flatly positive, 'That is false. Contact was made with two of our outer worlds. Your primitive craft was received with welcome according to our ancient tradition of hospitality to the stranger. Now they are sterile deserts. All life on those two worlds is extinguished.'

For Linden, the nightmare had begun again. Whatever he had done to clear his debt was long gone, swallowed up in this enormous catalogue of guilt. He stared wildly at Aarchon's face trying for some sign to believe that it was not true. Inexorably, the harsh voice went on, 'You came proclaiming peace, while you wrought utter destruction. Only a debased culture could perpetrate such an act of genocide.'

Linden's hands were covering his face. Koenig said urgently, 'Aarchon, you have to believe this. Such destruction was no part of Voyager's mission. It was launched with goodwill and the best of intentions.'

It made no impact. Aarchon might well have heard nothing. He went on with his brief. 'The High Council of the Federated Worlds of Sidon have determined it will not happen again. We have followed the primitive machine, Voyager One. As soon as we have located its source of origin, that planet and all living things upon it will be destroyed.'

Bergman and Helena Russell were aghast. Linden had slipped back into the state of shock which had followed his accident. Koenig said, 'That can only be for revenge. You use the word *primitive* freely enough. I tell you, revenge is the most primitive motive in the book.'

'We do not recognise this concept. The judgement of Sidon is unquestionable.'

Victor Bergman found his voice and picked up the point that was rankling him. 'You say we have a debased culture. Revenge sanctioned by authority is also a sign of a debased culture.'

'Argument is useless. Soon our fleet will be in effec-

tive range.' He paused, looked round the human faces
as though relishing the effect he was having. Annihilation
was one thing but they should savour it and go
through some mental anguish first. He turned the
screw another thread, 'Once we have determined the
location of Planet Earth your colony will be extinguished.'

Grim faced, Koenig said, 'These people have committed
no crime. We shall resist.'

Aarchon's bony head projected a chilling menace,
his confidence was absolute, 'Be warned. Nothing
you can do can change the judgement of Sidon. Resistance
will simply alter the manner of your destruction,
not the fact.'

Before Koenig could reply, the cube clouded,
becoming opaque again and the face was gone. The
cube elongated, narrowed to a glowing band, a bright
thread that dissolved and left them alone in Voyager's
silent command cabin.

Linden buckled slowly from the knees, arms clutching
at his chest and pitched full length to the deck.

Main Mission was dominated by the picture on
the big screen. Sandra had the three Sidon ships on
all the magnification she could get. Lean and powerful
they were a war party that looked well able to carry
out Aarchon's mission of destruction. But there had
to be something they could do.

Alan Carter at the Eagle Command console said
emphatically, 'We can't just wait. We can't stay on
our fannies like sitting ducks. I say we go out there
and hit them with everything we've got.'

Morrow had been studying the detail on the hurrying
spacers. 'They're *military* craft. Designed for war.
Your Eagles have a defence potential but they're
not in the same class. They don't have any sort of a
chance.'

Privately Koenig could go along with that and he could see that Bergman had the same opinion. But such defeatism would be likely to spread. Morale needed a booster shot action of some kind, however hopeless, and fast. Making his voice sound confident even to his own ears, he said, 'We're going to have a damn good try. They won't have it all their own way. Alan, move Eagles Four, Six and Ten to extreme intercept vectors.'

Reaction was immediate. He had pulled out of difficulties before and he would do it again. Carter's, 'Yes, Commander!' signalled a wave of optimism.

It was not shared by the man himself. Koenig turned away and went up the steps to his command office.

Helena Russell was, at the moment, detached from the battle. Patiently concentrating on her medical chores she was taking one thing at a time. She wrote up her log, checked the monitor readings on Linden's internal progress and stood by his bed, taking his wrist for a direct personal diagnosis.

The touch disturbed him. He opened his eyes.

'How do you feel?'

His voice was weak, hardly more than a whisper, 'Foolish . . . arrogant. For all those years I truly believed I had helped to push back the boundaries of man's knowledge. Now it has come to this!'

'Don't punish yourself. Many people have put science before responsibility.'

'I alone bear the responsibility for what Voyager did to the Sidons. Two worlds. Millions of dead. How can a man's mind accept that? It was never my wish to harm them. Believe me, I have never consciously wished harm to any man.'

'Doctor . . . the road to hell . . .'

'I know, paved with good intentions.'

He was becoming more agitated and she settled

112

him down. 'Relax. All that is academic now. Try to rest.'

When she left him his eyes were closed.

Victor Bergman had followed Koenig to his office. Meticulously squaring it off, he put a black box on the desk in front of the Moonbase Commander.

'Well, we have it John. What we tried for. That's the memory bank from Voyager. It's all there. Planets . . . compositions . . . life support estimates. I've not checked the half of it but it's packed with vital information.'

Koenig was looking at it but hardly seeing it. Helena Russell came in and stood quietly beside Bergman. Their eyes met over the box. Now there was no barrier between them. For him it was a personal gain which outweighed any data bank.

Still obsessed with his topic Bergman went on, 'The irony of it. All that information and we're not going to have the chance to use it.'

Koenig was seeing only Helena's neat head and the wide spaced, intelligent eyes. *There* was the loss if anywhere. Human identity was linked to a short fuse. He realised Bergman was talking and forced himself to listen. 'If you were a betting man, John, what would you reckon the odds? Fifty-fifty? Worse?'

This time Bergman got a reply. 'A thousand to one.'

'Against?'

'Against. But then I'm not a betting man, Victor. What we need is another chance.'

'You don't think Aarchon can be made to change his mind?'

'No.'

'How then?'

Koenig was speaking to Helena, 'Out of evil must come good. You have to believe that. There has to be a break out of the ring of violence. Destruction, killing, revenge. The cycle has to stop. Mankind knows that at heart. He always tries. Cries out for a second chance.'

'But how often has he got it?'

'Often Victor. Often.'

Bergman looked at him with affection. It was not scientific argument but it was a human one. He picked up his black box and went to the hatch. They were both quite still. As he went out, he said, 'Then I'll keep this. Just in case.'

In the absence of his medical jailer, Ernst Linden was ignoring her good advice. Biting his lips against the pain, he rummaged about for his uniform and zipped himself into it. There was a check while he searched for his commlock, then he was away for the hatch, anxious to be out before he could be stopped.

It took a while. Eyes clouded with pain, he saw two hatches side by side and had to wait, swaying on his feet until the attack passed and he could line up the commlock on the real panel. In the corridor, there was another hazard. Two security men approached and he had to straighten his back and make a normal casual walk. They passed. He was clear, but in an agony of pain. At the door of his experimental lab he had to stop again, hands flat to the wall. Then he was inside walking steadily past the duty technicians to his own restricted area.

The control device for Voyager was dark and silent; he sat himself at the console and hammered out a quick sequence. The circuit pattern came to life, glowing and pulsing. Linden waited, watching the power build, impatient to get on before he could be questioned. When he was sure, he made a slow deliberate job of a final sequence, tapping it out with neat, precise movements. Inside the command module of Voyager

One the control console flickered into action. Linden stood up slowly, looked round his workshop, drew his strength together and walked out the way he had come.

The technicians looked up to see him go, sensing something unusual. But there was no challenge. In the corridor again, he began to hurry, spurred by his desperate purpose, finding a nervous strength to move him on.

The detailed scan of the Sidon ships was crystal clear. Nerves in Main Mission were at a stretch. Koenig asked for a range figure and Paul Morrow read it off.

'Seventy-five thousand.'

Koenig said evenly, 'Eagles Four, Six and Ten. As soon as the Sidon ships are in range, open fire.'

Eagle Leader answered, 'Check, Commander. We're ready.'

They could only wait. Koenig turned to Carter, 'Every other Eagle on standby alert.'

'Have done, Commander.'

Helena Russell was looking for her patient. Standing by the empty bed she questioned Mathias, 'You say he's nowhere in the medical area?'

'Nowhere.'

'He could set himself back months. Get an all-sections call out.'

Jim Haines heard it in the experimental lab. He was looking incredulously at the pulsing circuit pattern when the announcer's voice from the communications post chimed with his thinking.

'All Alpha personnel. You are instructed to report the whereabouts of Doctor Linden. This is urgent.'

Haines was out at a run. He knew where Linden would be. Outside there was ordered chaos as the hive reacted and crews moved to the stand by Eagles. Haines checked launch pad signs and picked the one where Voyager had been berthed. He reached the intersection as Linden was two paces from the tube entry point and hurled himself forward to bar the way.

Linden was grey, almost finished. He said heavily, 'You're the last person who should try to stop me.'

'I'm not stopping you. I'm coming with you.'

It was a deadlock. Emotion choked Linden, he said, 'Jim. Please understand why I have to do this alone.'

Eyes held for a count. It was true. There was a kind of inevitable logic about it. Haines could not speak but he touched Linden's arm and stood aside.

Linden said simply, 'Thank you.' It was a quittance and a benediction. The hatch sliced open and he was through. It closed at his back and Haines was left staring at it.

When he reached Voyager One, Linden was calm, moving with new confidence. He knew now he would do what he had set out to do. He locked the hatch and seated himself at the command console under the scrawled names of his friends. He began to tap out an operating sequence.

In Main Mission Sandra Benes gave the latest range figure, 'Fifteen thousand.' But there was another claim to attention. Paul Morrow had seen a move from Voyager's pad and called urgently, 'Commander. Voyager One. She's taking off.'

It was true. They could now stop looking for Linden.

Koenig said, 'Linden!' and brought in the picture of the long silver ship lifting its nose from its temporary resting place. He called on the communications net. 'Linden. This is John Koenig. Do you read me Linden?' There was no response. Rocket motors flaring, Voyager One was jacking herself back into the element she had made her own. Koenig muttered furiously,

'What the hell is he up to . . . ?' and stopped, knowing the answer. It was Ernst Queller at the controls and he was gambling with the Queller Drive.

Sandra, as though hypnotised by the data she was getting went right on relaying it. 'Range ten thousand.'

Morrow said, 'I have a signal from Voyager One!'

'Range eight thousand.'

Koenig said, 'Linden!' and this time had a reply.

Infinitely tired but firm Linden said, 'Commander Koenig, activate all Alpha defence screens to maximum.'

'Are you crazy? We have no protection that can stand against that drive.'

'Recall all your Eagles.'

'They're all we have between us and the Sidons.'

'Do as I say and you might have a chance.'

The carrier shut off and Paul Morrow stated the obvious, 'He's broken the link.'

Bergman said, 'Do what he asks, John.'

Sandra chimed in with 'Range five thousand,' and the Eagle Leader said, 'All weapons locked, preparing to fire.'

Probabilities raced through Koenig's head but the decision was made out of conscious thought. He said sharply, 'Activate screens. Recall Eagles.'

'Range two thousand.'

Carter tried to reason, 'But Commander . . .' Koenig's voice lashed out, 'Do it!'

Carter called, 'Eagles Six, Nine, Ten. Return to Base.'

Eagle Leader was incredulous, 'But we have the range.'

'Return to base.'

On the big screen, there was a change, though nothing for the better. Aarchon's face was filling it from edge to edge, grim and foreboding. He said without preamble, 'John Koenig. You are wise to recall your primitive fighting craft. The manner of your destruction shall in return be merciful.'

Another voice answered him. It was Linden calling from his lonely post in Voyager One.

'Aarchon. Listen to me.'

Sandra split the screen and pulled him in so that Main Mission had a picture for the voice. Linden went on, 'This is Ernst Queller. I am the creator of the craft known as Voyager One.'

Aarchon said, 'What is the purpose of this, John Koenig?'

'Ernst Queller is acting outside my authority.'

Linden spoke again, 'Listen to me Aarchon. Your people have suffered grievous harm. But the blame is mine. Punish *me*. Do not condemn an entire world for the mistake of one man. My purpose was to unite a divided world, to reach out and follow a higher destiny into the infinity of space, to seek out other worlds and offer the hand of friendship.'

Aarchon was not impressed. He said coldly, 'There can be no discussion, Ernst Queller.'

'Hear me, Aarchon. Pride blinded me. Arrogance narrowed my vision. I and I alone was responsible for what my ship did. These other people are innocent.'

There was no change in Aarchon's face. Not even a pause as he said, 'Your plea is dismissed. John Koenig prepare to witness the judgement of Sidon.'

Linden was hunched over his console. With infinite sadness in his face and voice he said, 'Then you, Aarchon are no more worthy of life than I am.'

He looked up at the three names, put his hand to a lever and heaved it down. Voyager One's rocket motors cut out, she shuddered along her length and sprang forward with unbelievable acceleration into the path of the Sidon squadron.

Main Mission .was vibrating to its foundations. Aarchon's face on the scanner was distorted, whatever he was saying was unintelligible mush.

Morrow jerked out, 'The screens are holding!'

Bergman said, 'The Queller Drive. Linden's using it in short bursts. Look what it's doing to the Sidons.'

The area round the squadron was in a shimmer. Voyager One was streaking through like an arrow. Main Mission was vibrating again. Sandra had a confused picture on the screen. They could make out Linden using his last gramme of strength to punch a signal on his DESTRUCT panel.

Momentarily the picture held then it whited out into an asterisk of eye aching light. Voyager One and the Sidon squadron had vaporized as though they had never been. The rumbling and the vibration in Main Mission died away.

Jim Haines walked into the empty lab and stood by the work bench. The control circuit was dead, so much electronic junk. Balling a fist, he struck down at the flimsy structure, saw it shatter and missed the quiet step behind him that had brought Koenig to his back.

Koenig said, 'It did its work, Jim.'

Haines whirled round. 'What makes people tick, Commander?'

'Good question.'

'You work with a man. You think you know him. You come to respect him and suddenly you don't know him at all.'

'All that changed was the name. The man was the same.'

Haines stood digesting it and Koenig went on, 'Listen. His sacrifice gave us a future. His knowledge gave us hope. Someone has to carry on his work.'

He took the black box which he was carrying under his arm and held it out. 'If you respected the man make sure his sacrifice wasn't wasted. Here you are. Get to it.'

Haines watched him go. Then methodically he began to clear the bench.

CHAPTER SEVEN

John Koenig sat at his desk in the command office. It was one thing to have a unique file of useful information, it was quite another to have some way of manoeuvering their wandering Moon platform to some place where it would do good.

He checked himself. He was inviting trouble. Normality, when they had it was good enough. Through his observation window, he could see the orderly activity in Main Mission. Sandra Benes was doing a training session with a new recruit to the headquarter staff. Regina Kesslann looked as though she would be good. She was sensitive and quick to learn. That was something he had to think about. There was no foreseeable end to their journey. All personnel in senior posts should have a trained stand-in.

He saw Sandra look at the Main Scanner and take personal charge for a delicate piece of tuning. Their Moon was ploughing its furrow in an empty quarter. By some freak of chance that had to come up once in a while the scanner was a black velvet blankness, an empty slate for a cosmic figure to draw on. Even as he watched, he saw what had alerted Sandra begin to assemble itself out of nothing. Blackness was folding on blackness creating a spiralling mass that defied definition. It was the moment of creation over again. Where there had been nothing there was a primeval chaos, a spiralling mass that swirled at incredible speed and was suddenly alive with colour as tongues of incandescent gas spat from its spinning centre.

Red Alert klaxons sounded out through Moonbase Alpha and the hurrying moon seemed to side step in space. Loose gear slipped everywhichway and personnel caught off balance were flung to the deck. By the time Koenig had hauled himself into Main Mission it looked like a disaster area.

Helena Russell followed him in with Bergman only seconds behind her. Carter had a full set of executives for his report, 'Velocity increasing, Commander.'

Main Scanner had gone wildly out of focus and Koenig said sharply, 'Sandra?'

She was picking herself off the deck and took her seat at the console without a word. When the big screen steadied down there was a shocked silence. Edge to edge the frame was crowded with the most terrifying phenomenon they had seen. It was a churning vortex, shot with streamers of brilliant fire.

Paul Morrow said, 'Intense gravitational forces, Commander.'

'Computer analysis?'

Kano did his best, but the sensors were being overwhelmed. The computer made a start, but its overloaded circuits even failed to drop protection relays. There was a percussive crack and a thin plume of acrid smoke rose from between his hands. Hardly believing it, he said, 'Sensor relays gone.'

Carter was facing the same problem. He said urgently, 'Commander, velocity readings off the clock!' His console was pouring smoke as circuitry glowed cherry red. Sandra's desk was on the blink and Morrow reported again, 'All sensor equipment non op.'

The moon was accelerating, hurling itself forward into the unknown forces ahead. The outriders were already on them. Direct vision ports were suddenly flushed with colour, as tiny particles of exploding gas lashed them in polychrome rain. The whole fabric of Main Mission was creaking and groaning with stress like the timbers of a wooden ship in a hurricane wind.

The nightmare confusion was straining Regina Kesslann's yet untested inner strength. Hands rigid to her trim thighs, her mouth was open in a scream that melded into the racket like a piccolo entry. She saw Helena Russell and stumbled to her through the debris. As Helena took her hands trying to calm her, there was a dramatic change. All sound died away. The frenzied light storm ebbed to a white calm. They had reached the still dead centre, a timeless no-man's land.

John Koenig saw Bergman turning towards him in slow time as if in a dream sequence. His mouth was moving but only a distorted echoing sound was coming out. He saw Carter, also in slow time, the image wavering, soft focused, splitting slowly into two Carters. Panning round the control area, he could see the phenomenon repeated, Sandra and Paul Morrow were a wavering quartet, all four strained and pain wracked, holding their heads in intolerable agony.

Helena had taken the girl aside to a direct vision port. Outside, the moonscape was in a shimmer, wavering, splitting away, separating itself into two spheres that were sliding apart. She tried to alert Koenig and horror piled on horror. She had a choice. There were two Koenigs, both holding their heads.

Bergman was the same. Close beside her Regina was screaming again and wavering, fattening, sliding apart into two agonised duplicates. Then one peeled away and was gone, as her own agony built to a crescendo and she herself was tearing into a new creation. She saw Koenig's *doppelganger* wink out and leaned, sick and shaken against the glass, seeing and not seeing the duplicate moon accelerating away, hearing and not hearing Regina's ongoing scream.

Helena pushed off from the curving bulkhead like a swimmer making a turn and tried to cross the floor towards Koenig in a slow undulating run, hair streaming in a fair pennant.

Two steps from him, hand stretched out to him, she was gone in a white blank that spread until the whole of Main Mission was gone. Regina, running in panic fear from the exit was gone, Koenig was gone, Moon, space, time, all were gone.

There was no-one to see the Moon reform as a bright centre and the sky darken to velvet and the stars take up their station. It was all there unchanged and unchangeable as Koenig took charge of the cleaning up to get his station back on an operational footing.

Regina was the only one still unconscious and Helena, still shaky was working on her. Koenig looked questioningly at Mathias for a medical opinion.

'It's shock, Commander. We have six in the same state.'

'No other symptoms?'

'I can't be sure until they've been properly examined.'

Stretcher parties were moving in and Mathias went to superintend the operation.

Paul Morrow said, 'Internal systems seem to be in order, Commander.'

Koenig went on to the computer desk. Kano said, 'Sensor equipment took a beating, Commander. Every relay blown.'

'Take personal charge of repairs.'

Victor Bergman, still looking sick and shaken followed him on the tour and Koenig asked, 'What do you make of it, Victor?'

'I have no idea.'

On the scanner they could see that their moon had developed a comet tail of fine blue particles that gradually thinned out as they voyaged on over the star map. Koenig watched it for a moment then went on, completing his tour and finally moving out to check the state of the game in the medicentre.

Regina Kesslann was still unconscious, but what dreams she was having in the deep recesses of her head were not giving her any pleasure. Her young face was showing strain and a kind of terror.

Sitting on an adjacent bed, Helena said wearily, 'She doesn't seem to be responding to treatment John, have you any idea what happened to us?'

'Cause? None. Effects, well we all experienced them. Apart from some lingering shock and some memories of acute double vision and mental pain, there's only one real piece of evidence. We're in a totally different part of space.'

'It was all so . . . *real.*'

Koenig stroked her hair, 'Take some rest. Life goes on. We have a whole new set of possibilities.'

Back in Main Mission, he found Sandra Benes had a captive audience for the scan she was bringing up on the big screen.

She said incredulously, 'It's a solar system.'

Bergman said, 'Seems we've done a bit of travelling, John.'

Carter said, 'Some travelling Professor. Millions of kilometres in as many seconds.'

Koenig watched the star map vaguely troubled by it. He asked. 'How are the sensor repairs coming along, Victor?'

'Well on.'

Carter said, 'Even sensors won't tell us how we got here, Commander'

'True. But they will tell us what is in that solar system.'

Morrow said, 'Planets?'

'Could be. And more important, whether we could live on them.'

Last to rejoin the world of sense, Regina Kesslann opened her eyes in the medicentre and was some seconds establishing where she was. Helena, sitting at her desk was a touchstone and a familiar face to look at when she turned to check out the movement from the bed.

Regina's voice had its normal harmonics when she said, 'I had a bad dream.' But there was a change as she said, 'It's bright today, isn't it?'

'What is?'

Regina sat up, breathing suddenly irregular as a new panic seized her, 'Where am I? Please. I don't know where I am.'

Helena was beside her, 'Don't be frightened.'

'I was up there again. I saw it all. I saw two Moons. Alan was there. And the Commander. Everyone. You were there too. You were on that Moon. I *saw* you. It was a dream. Tell me it was a dream.'

'You must rest, Regina.'

'It was a dream. It couldn't be Alan and the Commander. They'll never come back. They're dead. Isn't the sun hot today?' She fell back on the pillow and began to cry in a silent grief that was real enough to her.

Helena Russell took a hypogun from her belt and gave her a sedative shot. Then she watched deep in thought, as the girl drifted into quiet sleep.

The repair work in Main Mission was ready for report. Koenig took it at his desk, as the executives put it on record.

Morrow said, 'Artificial gravity link up positive.'

Carter said, 'Velocity instrumentation okay.'

Kano called from his computer spread, 'Data systems functioning.'

Sandra said, 'Sensor relays repaired and checked.'

Carter was in again, 'Meteorite screens operational and on automatic.'

Paul Morrow looked over at Bergman, 'All output links-up completed.'

Bergman snapped shut a panel with an air of finality, 'I'm ready.'

Morrow put in the last link, 'Commander, all telemetric scanners are fully operational.'

'Fine. Open up. Everything we've got on that solar system.'

He left them to it, calling Bergman and Helena Russell into the command office for a conference on the more intimate problems of internal space. Maybe by this time they had some theory.

Victor Bergman leaned elbows on the table, spoke slowly, 'It's a familiar experience. Something we all know about. Déjà vu—the feeling that you've been this way before.'

'It's something more than that, Victor.' Helena was

positive. 'In Regina's mind, she's actually living on a planet, in open air, with sun on her face.'

Koenig asked, 'Does she know we're in a new solar system?'

'No. Her life here is somehow a bad dream to her—something she's been forced to come back to from somewhere else. You and Alan—I suppose that must be Alan Carter—are both dead as far as she is concerned. Whatever happened in that traumatic space storm, has affected her more deeply than anyone else.'

'We all shared the experience of seeing doubles of everything.'

'What I'm searching for is some way in which our experience of that phenomenon can relate to Regina's experience now.'

Bergman shifted irritably, not liking to be outside the limits of knowledge, 'We travelled way beyond the speed of light. How far beyond we can't tell. What happens to matter beyond the speed of light, we have no means of knowing.'

Koenig said, 'That used to fascinate me—the thought that if I could travel faster than light, I'd get younger, catch up on myself. I'd be able to look back on the life I'd just lived and live it again.'

Helena Russell gave him a wide eyed look and waited for more but Kano was in through the hatch with a print-out, looking astonished, saying, 'Commander!'

Koenig glanced at the text and was out of his chair in a smooth movement, racing for Main Mission with the others in his wake.

Carter was looking at the screen in disbelief, 'It can't be!'

Sandra Benes said, 'We've checked and double checked. There's no mistake.'

Trying to convince himself, Paul Morrow said slowly, 'Everything confirms it. All eleven planets check out.'

Koenig broke in, 'Paul. Use the long range scanner. Bring up the third planet. Kano. Get computer data on it.'

There was a pause. All eyes watched the screen. Computer's unemotional voice filled them in, 'Third planet. Distance from sun 148.8 million kilometres. Diameter 126,816 kilometres. Axial rotation 23 hours 56 minutes.'

Koenig said, 'Compare third planet to third planet in Earth's solar system.'

'Question illogical. Third planet is the third planet of Earth's solar system. The third planet's name is Earth planet.'

The screen was filled with the blue and white whorls of Earth planet. There was no longer any area of doubt. They had come home after their long wandering. It was their Ithaca.

Computer spoke again into the wondering silence, 'Moon velocity easing. Gravitational pull confirms moon going into Earth orbit.'

Patiently, Paul Morrow started over, 'Moonbase Alpha calling Earth. Come in Alpha Earth Control. Earth Control, do you read me? This is Moonbase Alpha calling Earth Control. Come in Earth Control . . .'

Only silence answered him and he went off on another tack, 'We are not receiving you, Earth Control. In the event that you are receiving this signal, we have computer forecast for re-entry into Earth orbit in forty-five hours.'

Kano said, 'Gravitational forces are compensating steadily. Shock wave conditions are not expected.'

Carter was jubilant, 'That's just great. We could take an Eagle down for a look right now.'

'But there is no response to our signals. I tell you something's wrong!'

'I say we should cut the talk and get moving. What's keeping the Commander?'

Behind his office door, John Koenig was fighting a rear-guard against conviction. He said to Bergman, 'Of all the billions of light years of space and after all we've been through, it just happens that we come through a phenomenon we can't begin to understand and find ourselves on *exactly* the right course to put us back *precisely* in orbit around the Earth? I can't accept it, Victor. I know less and less about this universe, but that *has* to be more than chance.'

'There is an underlying frame of order, John. We can kick it about from time to time. We can make stupid blunders like blasting ourselves out of orbit. But ultimately we belong where we belong. For us that's on Earth.'

Morrow blipped on the communications post, 'Still no contact, Commander.'

'Keep trying. I'll be right with you.' He looked at Bergman, 'What about that, Victor?'

'We've guessed at all kinds of disasters on Earth. Maybe we guessed right.'

In the medicentre, Regina was sitting up and taking notice. She looked more relaxed and at peace with herself. Helena Russell examined the fine smooth skin of her forearm and got a dazzling smile.

'It's only sunburn.'

'What sun, Regina?'

'What sun could it be? Up there.' She pointed a slim brown finger at the domed roof and went on, 'I think they've come back, that's why I'm feeling better.'

'Alan?'

'Yes, my husband and the Commander. Why have they been away so long?'

'You've been ill. Fever makes time seem like an eternity.' She paused, then went on, still fishing, 'I hadn't realised you knew him so well.'

Regina was suddenly agitated again, 'Where's Alan? Why doesn't he come to see me? He is here, isn't he?'

'Yes, yes he is.'

Regina tried to read Helena's face as though sure there was something being kept from her and her eyes filled with tears. Helena came to a decision, 'It's all right. Don't worry. I'll bring him to see you.'

The man himself was at the receiving end of a straight negative from Koenig.

'Look, Carter. If we go into orbit, we'll have all the time in the world for reconnaissance. But if you go down there now and for some reason we don't go into orbit, we'll have lost you forever.'

'But we *know* we're going into orbit this time Commander. Computer confirms it.'

'Computer's out of its depth in this situation, Carter. It knows nothing about it. Can it tell us why we get no signals?'

'No, Commander, it can't. That's one of the reasons why we should go down.'

'The answer's no. Not until we're safely in orbit.'

The communications post got Carter off the hook. The announcer said, 'Alan Carter to Medicentre please. Alan Carter to Medicentre.'

Koenig turned on his heel and walked up the steps to the command office. Paul Morrow gave Carter a friendly shove to get him started, 'They want you for a sedative, Alan. Cool you off a little.'

'That's all very well. Don't you people want to get home?'

Mathias had provided the star patient with a sketch block and it was paying off. Regina was calmer, rapidly filling page after page with bold simple drawings. Helena met Carter at the hatch and they walked together towards the bed.

Regina stopped drawing, stared fixedly at the paper as if suddenly frozen, then turned her head. Then the pad was flung aside and she was out of bed running with flying feet, calling, 'Alan!'

She threw herself on him, arms around his neck, head on his shoulder, sobbing as though her heart would break.

Alan Carter, totally bewildered tried to unlock her hands but could not, lifted her and carried her to her bed. Helena grabbed up a hypogun and gave her a sedative shot. Then it was over, she was away, limp and relaxed in instant sleep.

Carter straightened up, 'Will somebody tell me what that was about? I hardly know her.'

'She's living literally in another world. Sometime in her past or our future—if it is our future, it seems we evacuated Moonbase and went to live on a planet. We married, raised families. She was married to you.'

Alan Carter had gone on his knees beside the bed and was looking at Regina's calm, beautiful face. Deeply moved, he took one of her hands in both of his.

Helena picked up the sketch block and held it for him to see, 'I think Regina's other place is Earth planet.'

On the sketch, there was a strange geodesic house, flowers round it such as a child might draw and a large sun with fleecy stylised clouds.

Koenig had brought down the temperature in Main Mission and was going by the book, 'Still no response, Paul?'

'None, Commander.'

'What have we, Sandra?'

'Beyond simple magnetism and meteorological disturbance there is no source of electronic signal, Commander. None at all.'

'Victor?'

'We're building up a radio map. There have been some pretty major geological changes. The Earth's axis has moved by between five and six degrees, so climate conditions are totally altered.'

'And the people?'

'Complete disaster.'

'Paul, run a sweep for any signs of life.'

Koenig settled himself in the command seat. Personnel needed to know the score. He shifted a key and every communications post on Alpha had his picture. He said, evenly, 'Attention all sections Alpha. The Moon's velocity has stabilised. We shall shortly be activating the first phase of Operation Exodus. This is scheduled as soon as the Moon goes into Earth orbit . . .'

Regina Kesslann heard the transmission, stirred in her bed and sat up. The last words picked up echo, reverberated, filled her head with insane repetition. Sound was welling and pulsing all around her. Away beyond the foot of the bed she could see a mirror and an image that was unclear, but there was compulsion that she should go and look at it as though in some way it held the key to her dilemma.

Panic and fear surged through her mind, but she was out of bed, moving with small, reluctant steps until she was in front of it, eyes enormous, staring into it. Fear escalated. It was herself and it had been there waiting before ever she came near. She spun away, flimsy nightwear in a pale nimbus over smooth brown skin. There was another mirror carrying her image. She moaned like an animal in a trap, turned again to confront a third. She screamed, holding her head and the images watched her unmoved.

Now she was running from one to another. She hit one, stretched out her arms on the glass and stared at a big close up face that was her own. Her screams echoed and reverberated as she moved in a slow dream sequence as though each action had been slowed by a camera trick. Infinitely slowly her hands closed on a heavy paper weight on Helena's desk. Then she was striding in slow time to a mirror surface, beating at her own calm reflection.

Broken fragments floated out streaming past her as she turned away to meet Mathias coming in at a run.

With insane strength, she struck at him as he reached out to hold her and he fell away. She looked down at him, holding her head with both hands, sobbing in deep, painful gasps.

He lay still and she stumbled away for the door. It was closed and she scrabbled at the panels in a claustrophobic frenzy to get out.

She returned to Mathias. Looked with horror at his still body and forced her hands to take the commlock from his belt. Then she opened the door and ran out into the corridor, pain wracking her, moving jerkily in her floating flimsy wrap like a Maenad maddened and stung by an ivy leaf brew.

At an intersection, she had to stop, holding her head as unendurable pain reached a crescendo. She screamed out, 'Help me. Someone . . . please help me.'

A security man stopped in his tracks, whipped round and ran up to her. 'What is it?' He was reaching out to steady her, but pain needled her again and she twisted away moaning, 'Please, the pain . . .'

He tried again, aiming to pin her arms to her sides and carry her, but she was too quick. The commlock flailed down into the side of his neck and he dropped to the ground.

For a fleeting second she was herself again and knelt down beside him, overwhelmed by what she had done, flinging the commlock away in self disgust. But new surges of pain clouded her eyes and she began to moan. Hands that had meant to move on a mercy mission to try to undo what she had done, went instead to his belt and wrenched out his stun gun from its clip. Then she was away again on her insane, goaded run.

In Main Mission, there was an expectant hush as all hands watched planet Earth on the big screen. The moment of contact was almost due. They were waiting for Computer to pass its objective judgement.

Sandra said quietly, 'Five seconds,' and the counter clicked them off with a metallic click. Kano had linked for a visual print-out on the big screen and the words went across the blue planet like a seat of approval, 'EARTH ORBIT CONFIRMED.'

It got a spontaneous cheer. Paul Morrow and Sandra Benes were locked in a clinch. Every face was a smiling mask. Koenig had his hands on Helena's shoulders, saw his reflection in her wide eyes. But she was looking over his shoulder and her answering smile suddenly checked. She said, 'Regina!'

Regina Kesslann had appeared in the doorway of Main Mission. Hair dishevelled, head weaving from side to side, eyes wild with a panic fear she

134

could not control, a flimsily packaged nude, incongrously aiming a stun gun. Swaying on her feet, she said, 'Someone please help me.'

The change from euphoria took some seconds. There was no movement. She was alone in her closed ring of torment and called desperately, 'Alan!'

John Koenig and Helena moved together, running for the hatch. Helena stretched out her hand and said with gentleness and compassion, 'Regina . . . please . . . give it to me.'

Regina recoiled like an animal but what she said was two edged, asking and refusing, 'Stay away from me . . . help me.'

She looked wildly past them at Carter, 'Alan. Don't leave me again.'

Koenig said, 'Easy Regina. Take it easy. Give Doctor Russell the gun.'

Regina was past hearing. She evaded them, coming forward into Main Mission, moving erratically, pain rising in waves until her eyes closed and she screamed, 'Help me. My head. Please Alan!'

Koenig was close enough to try for the gun but extra sensory radar alerted her and her eyes opened. She said sharply, 'No,' and fired once over his head with a blast that shattered a bank of tell tales on the command console.

Helena said carefully, 'Regina,' trying to pack into it every soothing harmonic in her voice.

Regina said, 'I want my husband.'

She flung herself forward in a headlong run to Carter, reached him and was collapsing as her arms closed round his neck. Automatically he responded, holding her gently as her voice, tender and normal said, 'I knew you didn't die. I knew it.'

He opened her fingers and dropped the gun. She was still and quiet, then her back arched violently and her face creased in agony. She moaned, 'Alan!'

Her eyes were wide, staring. She was limp in his arms, all passion spent. He lowered her gently to the ground, white with shock, conscious that he had not been able to answer her appeal, knowing and not knowing that in some way he was involved. Helena Russell took a limp wrist to check pulse rate. There was no joy. Regina Kesslann was dead.

Bergman spread a colour chart on Koenig's desk. He tapped the area showing North America. 'The final survey comes out like this, John. North America's a desert. Arizona has Ice Age climate. These areas are nothing but radioactive ash. The only place where life can now exist is here. An area called Santa Maria.'

It was a lot to take in. Koenig's mind grappled with it.

'All those people . . . gone.'

'Let's hope some of them made it to Santa Maria.'

'All right, Victor. Tell Carter to prepare the Phase One Eagle for launch.'

Bergman nodded. There was nothing to say. The longed-for homecoming had gone sour. He went out and left Koenig staring at his chart.

He was still looking at it with unseeing eyes when Helena brought in an X-ray print. He said, 'Regina?'

She set it up for him on a scanner and even with his limited medical knowledge he could see what was impossible to believe. 'Two physical brains!'

'I thought I was dealing with schizophrenia brought on by the experience we all had. I had no idea there was an underlying physical condition.'

'Does it mean that what happened to Regina could happen again?'

'It happened to Regina. Why couldn't it happen to us?'

The communications post blipped and Morrow called 'Commander!'

On the big screen a halo of light was appearing from behind the Earth's mass. It was brightening like the sky after an eclipse. Another body was sliding out from behind the Earth's shielding bulk.

Koenig was in Main Mission, standing behind Sandra's chair saying, 'Increase magnification.'

'Maximum, Commander.'

The new feature was rising clear of the Earth. It was unbelievable. Paul Morrow said quietly, 'It seems we've gotten another Moon, Commander.'

There was no area of doubt. They had it clear and bold in sharp focus. A repeater on the communications console began to relay a weak single pulse signal.

CHAPTER EIGHT

Planet Earth had two Moons. They were both there, sharing the same sky. Personnel in Main Mission tried to adapt to it. At every desk there was a feeling of grim foreboding. They could go on, go through the motions, but the hopes they had cherished of the freak twist that had brought them home were so much Dead Sea fruit.

The weak signal pulse was bugging Koenig. He crossed to the main console and flicked switches.

A signal tone came in strength nine, identical in pattern. He looked hard at the duplicate Moon, 'That is our own navigation signal.'

Alan Carter said, 'Another Moonbase!'

Koenig nodded grimly, appalled by the implications that were crowding into his head.

Bergman said, 'Somehow, we've caught up with ourselves.'

There was a pause. Nobody moved. The navigation signal continued to beat, needling its message into every head. Koenig stirred himself, 'Postpone operation Exodus. First we have to find out what's on that Moon.'

Carter snapped into action, glad of something positive to do and called up the standby Eagle.

Koenig said, 'You and I, Alan,' and went for his gear.

Helena Russell, late on the brief, caught them at the boarding tube hatch, bulky anonymous figures and ran to them. 'John!'

He turned clumsily, visor hinged away. He was already out of reach in a human sense, a strange composite pachyderm. She stopped. It was no good. The logic of time was against them. She said simply, 'Be careful. Please be careful.'

Eyes made more sense, meeting, communicating a promise and a compact as far as anything was possible in the shifting quicksands they were in. He said, 'I'll do that. Don't worry, we'll be back.'

Then he was gone, with the hatch slicing definitively at his back and she went slowly to Main Mission to watch the monitor on the operations scanner.

Carter lifted the Eagle in a flurry of moondust, circled the base and headed out for the *doppelganger* Moon.

In a sense, it was home ground territory he knew

like the back of his hand. He took them in orbit watching the familiar moonscape peel away under the cone. He made a turn and a run over the old blackened waste areas and crossed low over Moonbase Alpha, no longer surprised at anything he might see.

Koenig looked at the complex. No light showed. It was deserted. He said shortly, 'Take her down.'

Carter turned, picked up navigation marks he had used on a hundred missions and brought them in to a perfect landfall with moondust rising in a grey cloud.

'We have no boarding tube, Commander.'

'Then we'll just have to walk.'

Koenig snapped shut his visor, waited for Carter and they both entered the lock. Outside, they were in swirling dust. Koenig pointed silently and they set off with a loping, low gravity gait. The single, repetitive signal was still sounding out, relayed by their communications packs.

They found a travel tube giving entry to the complex and forced open its hatch. Then they were moving in a darkened corridor, lit only by starlight from its direct vision ports. They passed the shell of a communications post, standing like a gaunt sentinel, all its equipment gone and reached Main Mission itself, a scene of empty desolation.

The signal went on, an insistent reminder of what had brought them to investigate. Koenig looked about him. There was one lunar clock, hands stopped. He said, 'Operation Exodus took place. Total Evacuation.'

'But when, Commander?'

'I don't know when. But I'll take a guess where to.'

He was standing at the main console looking over a piece of equipment and pressing dusty switches.

A slot in the main console opened grudgingly and extruded a cassette. The beacon signal stopped as he picked it out and Carter's voice cracked into sudden silence, 'Commander!'

Koenig joined him at a direct vision port and followed the line of his pointing finger.

A crashed Eagle was straddling a crater hollow on the perimeter of the base beside a sheer slab of lunar rock. There was something about it that drew them, something they both felt they had to see and they went out again, ungainly monsters in slow motion leaps, traipsing eerily over a technical graveyard.

The entry hatch was torn and hanging askew. They climbed into the passenger module in a faint cloud of floating dust. There was no time clock of corrosion to put a date on how long it had been there. It was timeless, a wreck in a silent sea with no crabs to home in its twisted fabric.

At each move, they disturbed more fine dust. Picking a way through crazily angled stanchions, they reached the command module hatch, which had burst from its frame and was hanging by a twist of metal. They leaned in and stopped. Evacuation Exodus had not been complete at that. The station had left its dead to keep an endless vigil.

There was an astronaut in each pilot seat; still strapped in place; fixed to look out over the Eagle's shattered cone to the domes and corridors of Moonbase Alpha.

Koenig climbed through, followed by Carter. He moved left to the dead co-pilot and stared at the visor. It was masked by a film of dust and he brushed it with his gauntlet, clearing a window, half knowing who he would find behind the glass. But the reality was still a shock and when Carter's face, set like a mask, appeared under his hand, he rocked back on his heels.

Carter himself was reeling away from the pilot seat, pointing in a mime for him to take a look. Koenig edged round in the confined space. Looked at Carter then down at the body he had been examining. There was a round clear space where Carter had brushed off the dust. He went closer to look inside. Through the two bubbles of glass, he was staring at himself.

He straightened up slowly. Whatever the situation, there was no doubt that he was still operating as a conscious agent. I think, therefore, I am. There could be information to be had from these deaths. Whether one was his own or not was irrelevant. He said, 'All right, Alan. Get the harness off them. We're taking them back.'

Laid out on examination tables in the Medicentre's special diagnostic unit and bathed in a soft light from the decontamination filters, the dead could have been asleep.

Helena Russell wearing a white mask, drew the sheet to cover Carter's face and moved over to Koenig. The sleeping and the dead. Where was the secret of the inner flame that made a person? Deep in thought, she did not hear the hatch open and when Koenig spoke she shuddered as though the words had come from his dead lips.

'How did we . . . they . . . die?'

She looked from the dead face to the living and went to meet him. 'Something like five years ago their Eagle crashed on the Moon. They were both killed instantly on impact.'

'They've been there five years?'

'Yes. Preserved unchanged by the space vacuum.'

'You know there's only Santa Maria as a habitable site for the rest of the Alpha people, if they are still alive?'

'I believe they are. Regina was trying to tell us that all along.'

'We'll soon know.'

'You're going down there?'—she was resigned to it, but there was no doubt she expected the worst.

'Yes. I've activated operation Exodus.'

'We've seen what happened to Regina as soon as we came into Earth orbit. It could happen to all of us.'

'Why hasn't it?'

'Regina was hyper sensitive.'

'And you believe that the nearer we get to Earth and these other people . . .'

'Not other people—our other selves, John.'

'It could happen again?'

Memory of the still form under the sheets was vivid to her and she could not look at him, knowing he would read the fear in her eyes. She put her head on his chest and very gently he stroked the silky pad of hair under his chin. He said, 'Don't answer that. What has to be, will be. We're not finished yet. I have to go, they'll be almost ready in Main Mission.'

Operation Exodus was moving inexorably through its stages, with timed announcements on the general net. Main Mission personnel were manning all desks for the rundown. Bergman watched the other Moon, still the dominating feature on the big screen. He was fascinated and repelled by it. He could not leave it alone. He said, 'Give me all the magnification you can get.'

He stared closely at the well known features, made calculations on a loose pad and crossed thoughtfully to Kano at the computer desk. 'Run that through.'

Kano accepted it without a word. For him, it was so much water under a bridge. They were leaving. One Moon, two Moons. He would settle for a half dozen if it got him to Earth planet. He looked at the figures, translated them for computer pillow talk and keyed them in. The print-out was almost instantaneous and Bergman ripped it off.

Carter, who had been watching the operation, joined him. Bergman said slowly, 'It's increasing velocity.'

'That's not possible.'

'Nevertheless, that is what is happening. It's closing on us rapidly.'

'How rapidly?'

'If its present velocity is maintained, both Moons will collide in thirty-six hours.'

John Koenig and Helena had gone through into the command office. Helena was staying close, as though she knew that their future together was balanced on a knife edge. Koenig called Bergman, 'Have we enough time for the Phase One probe?'

Bergman checked his calculations, 'You will have only ten hours on the surface. We'll need a full twenty-four hours for Phase Two . . . total evacuation.'

Looking at Helena, Koenig said, 'Activate Phase One, as of now.'

He was on his way, cutting through all the mental doubts and reservations by simple physical action. But Helena had reacted faster and was between him and the hatch. Hands homed gently on his chest. He stopped. Other than trampling on her, he had no alternative. He said, 'Don't you see? We have no choice. If we don't get off this Moon now everyone will die anyway.'

He tried to pass, but she still held him. She said 'Then only you and Carter must go. Your other selves died in another place. There should be no danger to you.'

Koenig considered it. There was some other angle

and he tried to find it but her eyes were clear and frank. She went on for the punch line, 'And I must come with you.'

It was out of the bag and he tried to think of the consequences for her. Carter and himself might well have a ticket for a death at another place and another time, but she had no such guarantee.

She could read his mind and went on, 'I have to go. Medically, we must know what is to happen.'

He could have said that Bob Mathias would do the mission just as well but the pass had been sold where intellectual logic chopping could not reach. He wanted her with him for the last hours. She was determined to be with him. How could he stop her?

He slid his hands under the silky bell of fair hair, touched her forehead with his mouth. They went out together walking soberly for the waiting Eagle.

Carter in the pilot seat gave them a thumbs up signal and Koenig left him the command module to himself. He took Helena through into the passenger module. The boarding tube snaked away, Carter gunned the motors and lifted the Eagle in a surge of power like a free standing elevator.

Through the vision ports, they could see the Earth, screening its ravaged surfaces in bland cloud. They could also see their two Moons racing on a collision course that no power could stop.

Koenig knew she was watching him and looked at her. Her eyes were enormous, almost all pupil, avenues to enter and wander in, accepting, affirmative.

He said, 'What is time? Only the knocking of a subjective clock. If we say so, the seconds can be hours, the minutes years.'

They heard Carter calling Moonbase Alpha. He said, 'Eagle on course for Santa Maria touchdown.'

Morrow's voice answered, 'E.T.A. 0400 hours Earth time. Good luck, Alan.'

Helena's voice was hardly above a breathing whisper, 'On that calculation we have a lifetime before Alan takes us down. How shall we spend it?'

Her lips were soft as unseen moss, an open O, dissolving, slightly salt. Their hurrying module was nowhere, a place of meeting outside space and time. The truth was a revealed thing to Koenig. There was nothing in the whole spread of the Universe that mattered to them as human beings, except what happened between a man and a woman. They were the still centre of the turning worlds.

He was wise enough not to try to put it in words. Words were not necessary between them. They were on the same side of the equation. Mc^2 equals love.

In Main Mission Sandra Benes said emotionally, 'They're on their way to Earth!'

Bergman said, 'And going back into a future time. It's an interesting thought.'

The Eagle was approaching Earth. Carter delayed heat shields. As they hit the outriders of the atmosphere, the Eagle glowed symbolically like a shooting star.

Dust jetted in a hurricane storm round the landing Eagle, shrouding it in double darkness. Dawn was not far off. The Earth's two moons and a scatter of stars gave some light as the dust settled uneasily.

Carter gave them a little more time, slowly unbuckling his harness and leaving his console ready for a crash lift off. When he went through into the passenger module they were preparing to go out.

Koenig paused with his hand on the hatch lever. It was now. The interlude was over.

He said, 'All right?'

Helena's steady 'Yes,' touched his heart. He pulled

down the lever and shoved open the hatch. They stood looking out at a darkened wilderness.

A dawn wind sighed, lifting spirals of dust. There were shadows folding on to themselves and the stark outlines of small stunted trees. He jumped down, held his arms for Helena and swung her out beside him. Leaving the Eagle, they struck out for the nearest man made artefact which looked, in silhouette, to resemble the top of a satellite control tower.

When they reached it, there was no area of doubt. The top twenty metres stuck up out of ashy soil.

Koenig said, 'It's the Santa Maria satellite tower.'

Helena said, 'John, there was a whole community of fifty thousand people. This tower is hundreds of metres high.'

'Ash to this depth, what could have happened?'

Carter had gone ahead and appeared out of the darkness, 'Commander, there's a settlement quite close. The houses, would you believe it, they're the split image of what Regina was drawing?'

They followed him round the tower to the crest of a rise and below them the settlement was spread out. The builders had gone for geodesic dome structures based on triangular units for strength. Some windows were showing flickering yellow light like a warm candle glow.

As a defence against wind erosion, the settlers had planted a screen of low bushes on the perimeter of the cultivated area and the three Alphans stopped, suddenly aware that strangers approaching in the night might not be welcome.

Koenig said, 'You two go round and start from the other end of the settlement. I'll work down from here. We'll play this very slowly.'

Koenig went forward, feet sinking in soft ash. He was twenty metres from the nearest dome on his side when a hatch opened and light spilled out. A figure robed like a monk appeared momentarily in silhouette and was gone as the door shut at its back.

Koenig saw it again, moving his way and stayed still. In spite of the earliness of the hour, whoever it was was in a cheerful mood and was whistling quietly to himself. It was a routine check on something growing in the ashy soil. The figure bent down, examined a plant, straightened and came on.

The tune was plain now. It was Beethoven's 'Ode to Joy,' a tribute to optimism if ever there was and gave Koenig an identity clue.

The figure reached a small cleared area and straining his eyes, Koenig could make out the form of a swivel mounted optical telescope. There was no doubt it had to be Victor Bergman, still batting and using what scientific gear he had been able to salvage.

Bergman was clearly puzzled. Only one Moon was visible. A cloud bank had drifted over the other. But he was not happy with the one he had. It seemed to be in the wrong place. Obviously puzzled, he was turning about, searching the night sky.

He swung the telescope, trained it on the cloud bank and was looking through it as the clouds drifted clear and the Moon he was looking for was staring down at him.

Koenig came forward, heard Bergman say, 'It's happened!' and was suddenly in his range of vision as though he had risen from the ground.

Bergman said, 'You've come back.' There was no surprise in it. Just a flat finality. It was a statement, without any harmonics of welcome.

Koenig said, 'Yes. We're back.'

Alan Carter and Helena were cautiously approaching a geodesic dome at the far end of the settlement. There was some light from inside. Some at least of the struggling community were early risers.

Carter motioned for Helena to stay back and went forward himself to look through a window.

It was a scene as old as time, in spite of the sophisticated building techniques of the dome. Two women were preparing food on a stone built range. There was a round vessel blowing a plume of steam. They wore simple tunics. One was facing him and although she looked older, there was no doubt about identity. He was looking at Sandra Benes.

The other woman straightened from the stove, walked to the table and turned her head. She was looking directly at his window and his reaction triggered sudden alarm in Helena. 'What is it?'

She moved beside him and he tried to stop her from looking in. But she was insistent. Whatever it was, she had to know.

It was herself. Older, with lines of suffering around the eyes, dressed in a simple, one piece robe, she was there, living another life. A life where John Koenig had no place. A life where he was dead, strapped in a wrecked Eagle on an empty Moon.

It was too much to bear. She said, 'Alan!'

The older Helena had sensed that something was strange. The slight noise confirmed it. She stared hard at the window, seeing her own reflection and then knew it was all wrong. No glass could be as flattering and peel away the years. Horror and realisation dawned on her. She fought a rearguard, trying to keep calm but it was too much. Panic pushed her over the edge and her mouth opened in a scream that died away as her mind blanked. She fell on her knees and folded to the floor.

Pausing only to activate an alarm lever, Sandra rushed to her. She saw the younger Helena's face still at the window and a sudden terror held her, open mouthed and very still.

Keyed to the alarm, flood lights blazed out on the compound. Blinded by the sudden glare, Carter and Helena had hands to their eyes as they stumbled clear of the dome.

When they could see, the area had come alive. They were close to a small area of cultivated garden. The property owners were turning out to defend their hard won clearing in the desert. Morrow, Kano, Tanya. All carrying stun guns.

Wakened by the alarm, there was the high wail of a child crying.

The Earth people moved up close. There was no pleasure or welcome in their faces. It was a hostile, defensive group, ready to fight for what it held.

Bergman and Koenig ran up and Paul Morrow, falling back on a formula from the past said, 'Commander Koenig!'

Koenig said, 'Paul! Kano!'

The sun began to edge its way over the bleak horizon. It showed up the extent of their empire. It was pitiful. A finger-hold clawed in barren rock.

Koenig sat on Bergman's cleared patch near his telescope and tried to think it out. Two children ran from a dome, came towards him and stopped, fascinated by what they knew was strange and very fearful.

Koenig called them. It was enough. They were away like rabbits to a safe burrow. Bergman joined him.

Bergman was the only one still trying to find a way for them to live. He said, 'How do I begin to make them understand?'

'Have you tried?'

'Effectively I told them a true ghost story and they couldn't resist the temptation to come and look at a living ghost.'

'They look fine kids.'

'They are. That's our finest achievement.'

'Whose are they?'

'Sandra's and Paul's. The children are our future. As our situation improves, there will be more.'

'That's a tremendous challenge. To bring back life to a dead world.'

'It hasn't been easy. It has meant total recycling of all our resources. Eagles. Life support systems, fuel sources. That's why you could not contact us. We have used everything there was to make this place habitable.'

'It works.'

'It was a choice, a decision we had to take at the beginning. If we failed, that was it. There could be no second try.'

'I think it was a wise decision.'

'You should know. You made it.'

Paul Morrow was showing Carter a flower strewn patch with a headstone incised by laser beams. It read REGINA CARTER. He said, 'There was a terrible electric storm, as though comets were fighting over the sky. Regina suffered most. Six days later she was dead.'

'That was when we came into orbit. Our Regina died too. Both at the same time.'

'Not a coincidence.' He looked at Carter, face hard and unsympathetic.

Helena Russell came to a sudden decision and pushed open the door of the living unit, where they had taken her other self. The older woman was lying on a daybed and opened her eyes, full of strain and fear.

Helena said gently, 'I'm sorry if I frightened you.'

There was no help from the figure on the bed. She continued to stare.

Helena went on, 'It must have been a tremendous shock. I knew something about what to expect. You didn't know?'

'No. Are we really the same person?'

'We were the same person once. Now we live in different times at the same time.'

'But not in the same place. We can't!'

'We have no choice. It's something we must all come to terms with.'

The older Helena struggled to sit up, trying to flight off the fear that was in her eyes. 'You must leave. I have my own life. I have accepted it. I have my work. It is enough.'

'But I won't interfere with your life. We can help each other. We can all help each other.'

'Is everybody up here?'

Helena knew what was behind the question. 'Yes.'

'John Koenig?' It was out in the open, the real point of issue between them.

She hesitated, then said calmly, 'Yes.'

'John Koenig was my husband.'

'How could I know?'

'He'll come here, won't he?'

'He'll come. None of us can choose. Our Alpha is close to destruction.'

Earth Helena was showing signs of agitation, voice in rising hysteria, she demanded, 'How can we live together? You and John Koenig. You with my husband. How can I come to terms with that?'

There was a change. She was listening intently and said suddenly, 'He's here now. I know it.' She was off the bed, running for the door.

Helena threw herself forward to block the way, said, 'No, you mustn't!'

But she was flung aside as the other woman rushed blindly out of the dome.

A rising scream alerted Koenig and Bergman. Helena and Sandra ran out of the house and stopped. Carter and Morrow turned from Regina's grave, Kano, Tanya and the children ran to see. Every eye tracked Earth Helena as she ran on a weaving, erratic course to Koenig and clung to him in a wild passion. Koenig could only respond, face grave and compassionate. Over the shaking shoulder his eyes met those of his time peer Helena. The situation was outside every scheme of reference. How could they handle it?

Earth Helena suddenly went limp, head arched away from him, only held up by his supporting arms. Tenderly, Koenig lowered her to the ground. Her eyes were fixed, he reached out and closed her eyelids. For her at least, the dilemma was resolved. She had seen him back from the dead, had touched him and had died.

Slowly and sadly he stood up. Others moved in to carry her away. He would have helped, but Bergman said sharply. 'All right. Leave her. We'll take care of her. She is one of us.'

They had the open ground to themselves. The settlers had withdrawn. Helena was inconsolable.

Koenig said, 'You mustn't blame yourself, Helena.'

He had never seen her look more vulnerable and defeated. She refused to be comforted, 'The whole thing is impossible.'

'You're wrong. We *have* to make it work.'

Alan Carter alerted them, 'Commander!'

The whole community had turned out and was approaching them. It was a hostile tribe defending its territory. They had come round to a majority verdict. They were rejecting their strange counterparts as alien and menacing to their way of life.

Helena moved closer to Koenig. Carter drew his stun gun.

Koenig spoke out, 'We have no choice. The Moon will be destroyed in the collision.'

Earth Morrow said tightly, 'Go back to your own place, Commander. We've fought hard for our life here. We have children. We have a future. We will not let you destroy it.'

Koenig said, 'We can build somewhere else. We have exactly what you had to start with.'

'No. It won't work. Take your people and go back.'

Koenig turned deliberately to Carter, 'Alan. Call Moonbase. Tell them to activate Operation Exodus immediately.'

Morrow had worked close. As Carter sheathed his gun and opened his commlock, Earth Morrow threw himself forward and grabbed for it, wrenching it away and bringing up his own gun to threaten them.

Bergman, torn by indecision had been at the back of the group and ran forward. He shouted, 'Wait.' He had the centre ground and they all listened as he went on rapidly, 'Regina died because she came face to face with herself in her own mind. Helena confronted herself in the flesh and our Earth Helena could not live. If the rest of us were to come together, the result could be chaos and disaster.'

He paused to steady himself and went on earnestly, 'But for another, more logical, inevitable reason, coexistence is impossible. We belong to different times. When those two Moons collide, time will correct itself. Normality will return. One Moon. One set of people. In other words, our communites will cease to exist in the same time. You must go back.'

Carter said, 'Back to what? Certain death?'

'If you're not there when time corrects itself, you'll have nowhere to die.'

There was silence. He had made his point.

Helena said wearily, 'Take us back, John. Our time and our place are on Alpha.'

The whole community watched them go. There was no move and no farewell as the Eagle blasted itself out of its dust cloud and Carter wheeled it away in a long climbing turn. They watched it diminish to a distant speck on their empty horizon. The mournful, sighing wind was the only sound in the ash desert.

Carter took them in to their home Moon with the time freak Moon closing in and their destiny for good or ill waiting in the wings. In the passenger module, Helena and Koenig sat side by side. As they touched down, she lifted a small bunch of fresh flowers she had taken from the Earth garden.

Koenig was proud of his people. He looked round Main Mission and checked them off. Morrow and Sandra, Carter at his operations desk, Kano, Tanya, Bergman, Helena herself at the observation gallery looking out. They were rock steady. Tense and quiet but ready to take what had to be.

The moons were closing, beginning to overlap. Chaos had come again. Main Mission was lashed in lurid, flashing light that drove Helena back from her window. The whole fabric of the base was groaning and wrenching at its foundations. The huge, churning mass of tormented space was all round them.

Sandra staring hypnotised at the big screen was overwhelmed, her despairing scream was soundless in the tumult that engulfed them. Then she was gone and Main Mission was whiting out in blinding eye-aching light.

Koenig gripping his desk until his knuckles showed white, hauled himself to his feet and looked for Helena. She was still near the window looking out and then she was gone. It was all gone. There was only the centre of white light pulsing and throbbing like a monstrous heart beat.

None of them saw the Moon reappear from the great welter of cosmic force and sail out from constellation to constellation, moving faster than any instrument could measure or any mind understand.

Then the insane racket died away, the space sky had stabilised around them. The main scanner was a black velvet pad. Personnel were standing up, looking around to see if they were alone as a wandering Ka or if what they saw was real.

Koenig ran up the steps to find Helena. She was holding her bunch of Earth flowers. She said, 'It's over. We've come through, John.'

Sandra called, 'We're in different space, Commander.'

They were all wanting his opinion. He still had a command and a job to bring them home somehow, somewhere.

Carter said, 'I wonder if the others made it, Commander. If they survived?'

Victor Bergman asked, 'Did they really exist?'

Koenig had an arm round Helena's shoulders. He could settle for that. She was alive. Whether the others were there in their slot in the future was an academic issue. Good luck to them anyway if they were.

He said slowly, 'Maybe they are saying the same thing about us?'

Helena was more sure, she looked at her flowers, 'They did exist. They were real.'

John Koenig sat at his command desk. He felt the edge of it hard and solid against his hand. Around him, Moonbase Alpha was stirring like a busy hive, repairing itself, making good, holding their life support systems together. The Moon ploughed on over the endless star map. Somewhere, there would be a landfall.

Helena had left him her flowers in a plastic beaker. He looked at them. They were already beginning to wither. He swivelled away from the desk, stood up and went to find her.